THE

Mark Marinovich has captured the essence of the sea for anyone to savor in *The White Boats*, about a spunky boy who lives in the Baja and dreams of catching a blue marlin. Against great odds, the boy follows his heart and attempts to save an entangled humpback whale. Enjoy *The White Boats* with a pinch of salt and a squeeze of lime. Bravo.

Jim "Homer" Holm
Executive Director, Clean Oceans International

Single-use disposable plastics in the sea know no boundaries. Therefore we must stop the spigot of plastic pollution entering the marine chain each and every day on a global scale. In *The White Boats*, Cesar comes face to face with the true cost of marine plastic as he struggles to free an entangled majestic humpback whale from a fatal plastic fate. Refuse disposable plastic daily.

Dianna Cohen
CEO and Co-Founder, Plastic Pollution Coalition

The White Boats reminds us that there is no "away," and that everything flows downstream, and downstream is the ocean. Cesar's awareness and drive to take action as a youth who can see something wrong in his surroundings, will hopefully inspire many others to do the same in their own communities. Plastic pollution is one of the biggest challenges of our time, because it is so challenging to recover, and also get rid of. *The White Boats* is an exciting story of the interaction with humans and the sea, with an environmental message for all ages to embrace.

Doug Woodring
Founder, Ocean Recovery Alliance | Global Alert Platform

A gripping story that I couldn't put down. *The White Boats* covers ocean plastic pollution, the power of idealism, poverty, drug cartels and more, with some humor thrown in. A fun and eye-opening mythic tale.

Hallie Austen Iglehart
Founder, All One Ocean: Making Every Day Beach Cleanup Day
Author, *Womanspirit* and *The Heart of the Goddess*

"We're all in this together" is the powerful message from *The White Boats*. Mark Marinovich's exciting narrative highlights the mission to educate as well as to take ACTION on the serious global problem of marine debris.

Michael David Loftin
Executive Director, 808 Cleanups

The White Boats is a compelling tale that involves an all-to-common, real-life problem: the entanglement of a humpback whale in human-generated debris. The novel's young man of the sea is a true environmental hero whose story is a real page-turner. I highly recommend it!

Dan Haifley
Executive Director, O'Neill Sea Odyssey
Former Executive Director, Save Our Shores

In a world where issues like litter and ocean pollution can be totally overwhelming for the individual, *The White Boats* gives hope that a single person can make a huge difference. Yes, marine debris is an international issue, but its solution starts with each person making a choice to make the world a healthier place and that the next generation is the key, just like Cesar's grandfather predicted.

Heidi Taylor
Managing Director, Tangaroa Blue Foundation

Those who are involved in the journey of raising awareness about plastic pollution experience an all too familiar apathetic view towards the ocean on a constant basis. Finding creative and entertaining ways to turn apathy into empathy is a continual struggle. But after reading *The White Boats*, the arsenal of awareness-raising methods was armed with a new tool. This entertaining and inspiring novel entangles you like a net and doesn't let go until you, yourself, are set free. This page turner/swiper leaves the reader with hope for the future of our oceans and the desire to be part of the solution.

Kahi Pacarro
Executive Director, Sustainable Coastlines Hawaii

I introduced my two grandchildren to 10-year-old Cesar, the hero of *The White Boats*, and they were entranced by Cesar's daring and bravery when he encountered the whale caught in fishing net. Walking along our local beach the next day, they talked about Cesar and his grandfather collecting litter, and they filled a shopping bag with plastic and brought it home for recycling.

Michelle Renshaw
Author and Historian

From generation to generation, the good, the bad and the ugly of our world is passed down. What we do today will make a difference tomorrow and this is captured uniquely in the inspiring tale, *The White Boats*. Inspiration for so many campaigns come from our youth, yet the wisdom of our ancestors is encrusted in the driving forces that power these unique individuals. In this story, Cesar learns from his grandfather and uses his divine power to drive a message our world needs to hear. A captivating read with a powerful message, Mark has written with an obvious passion and the message is clear: *Clean Oceans Make Us All Winners.*

Ian Thomson
Founder, Ocean Crusaders

I was engaged from the first page of *The White Boats*. Cesar's determined struggles to achieve a dream show the endurance of the human spirit to make right the wrongs in this world, even when it seems impossible at times. The enormously complex global issue of marine debris (or better phrased, "human-made plastic pollution") is an issue that threatens to impact man and sea creatures alike. Slowly the conversation is heating up and we are at a junction in time when it is not too late. We applaud Mark for writing a book that addresses an issue that all countries must confront.

Amanda Marechal
Co-Founder, Take 3

In *The White Boats*, Mark Marinovich not only tells a captivating story about a young boy's aspirations, adventures, and struggles; he also manages to weave in messaging about environmental sustainability and conservation throughout the novel. Cesar and his grandfather's determination to curb marine plastic pollution will inspire readers to do their own part to prevent plastic pollution and protect the ocean, no matter where they live. Readers can get involved in a variety of ways, including by joining together with others around our blue planet to celebrate World Oceans Day in June.

Bill Mott
Director, World Oceans Day | The Ocean Project

Fishing communities have a front seat to the increasing devastation that plastic pollution and other insults have on our oceans. In *The White Boats*, Cesar, a young hero, joins others in the conviction to eradicate the blight of plastic pollution from the marine environment. In an inspiring act, he risks his life to save a whale that is ironically tangled in plastic fishing net. The people, and especially the youth, who live close to the ocean are the hope for its future.

Georgienne Bradley
Director, Sea Save Foundation

THE
WHITE
BOATS

A NOVEL

MARK MARINOVICH

Foreword by Melati and Isabel Wijsen

Palancar Press

Names: Marinovich, Mark.
Title: The white boats / Mark Marinovich.
Description: Capitola, CA : Palancar Press, 2016.
Identifiers: LCCN 2016914388 | ISBN 978-0-9980664-0-0
    (pbk.) | ISBN 978-0-9980664-1-7 (Kindle ebook)
Subjects: LCSH: Fishers--Fiction. | Courage--Fiction. | Hu-
    man-animal relationships--Fiction. | Plastic marine debris--
    Environmental aspects--Fiction. | Baja California (Mexico :
    Peninsula)--Fiction. | Bildungsromans. | BISAC: FICTION
    / Action & Adventure. | FICTION / Coming of Age. |
    GSAFD: Bildungsromans. | Adventure fiction.
Classification: LCC PS3613.A74876 W58 2016 (print) | LCC
    PS3613.A74876 (ebook) | DDC 813/.6--dc23.

Palancar Press
Capitola, California 95010
PalancarPress.com

10 9 8 7 6 5 4 3 2 1

No bleach, chlorine, acid or plastic was used in the manufacture
of this book.

Printed in the U.S.A.

Foreword

Plastic has only been on Earth for around 100 years, but it has taken over the average daily lifestyles of Earth's human inhabitants. Did you know that we use a plastic bag for just thirty minutes on average? Yet it continues to exist in nature for thousands of years after we discard it! Every single piece of plastic that has ever been produced still exists today.

In Bali, Indonesia, where we live, plastic was introduced only 20 or 30 years ago. Before plastic arrived, our community in Bali relied purely on nature itself. Today, Bali is still a paradise, but one that is awash in plastic trash. Having been born and raised on the island, Bali is our home—we love it and we want to take care of it. Even as 10- and 12-year-olds we knew something had to change. Plastic was everywhere.

That is when it all started. In 2013, we kicked of our campaign called "Bye Bye Plastic Bags," a youth-driven social initiative to get the people on the island of Bali to say no to plastic bags. Since then we have been on a mission with 25 or 30 kids from both local and international schools to ban plastic bags on our island. It hasn't always been easy, but because of our commitment and persistence we have achieved a lot, from winning awards to working closely with government bodies to a recent global TED talk in London.

But our biggest achievement so far is getting the support and commitment of the government to make Bali plastic bag-free by 2018.

The time for change has never been better than right now. And change is happening. People are starting to be more conscious and aware, and they are sharing their knowledge in every way possible. We need to keep sharing and keep educating because this is how change begins.

We are endlessly grateful for *The White Boats*, a wonderful novel by Mark Marinovich, in which he shows the urgency to act and offers solutions that we can carry forward. Most importantly, we are grateful for the youth empowerment that Mark highlights throughout his book, something that we connected with the most in his story, next to the plastic problem. He strongly portrays the power we have as youths and that we can make a difference, no matter what our ages are. We kids may only be 25% of the world's population, but we are 100% of its future.

Keep this question in mind while reading *The White Boats*: Is plastic really the legacy we want to leave behind for future generations? And if not, what are you going to do about it?

Melati (age 15) and Isabel Wijsen (age 13)
Co-founders, Bye Bye Plastic Bags
Bali, Indonesia

August 2016

1

All that remained of Cesar's deep sea fishing magazines after he cut out all the pictures were words he could not read. The excised pictures, of blue marlin leaping, twisting and fighting hooks and lines of unseen anglers, ringed the walls of his small gray cinderblock room. The ocean horizon in each image was carefully aligned with the next, creating a continuous panorama. The boy yearned to catch a blue marlin of his own. He would release his trophy catch to fight another day, but before he released the fish he would capture it again with a photo, just as they did on the white boats, and he would add his blue marlin to the wall. Soon, he thought.

Cesar lay on his bed—a narrow plywood board spanning two stacks of cinderblocks and padded with foam rubber—and thumbed through a deep-scissored magazine. Declining daylight backlit a faded floral curtain in his bedroom's small window. An overhanging light bulb provided the only other light.

In the next room his mother, Rosa, and an unfamiliar male voice were locked in a heated quarrel that buzzed through the boy's delaminated hollow-core door.

Cesar tossed the magazine on the floor, unplugged the bare bulb, and buried his head under a sarape that served as sheet, blanket and pillow. The late Baja evening was hot and would still be hot for several hours. Cesar, wearing only jeans, flung the sarape aside and cupped his hands over his ears.

A shadowy form in a high corner of the room twitched and drew the boy's attention. Cesar made out the contours of a scorpion that had found an unsealed fold in the corrugated metal roof. The arthropod's claws stretched wide and a segmented tail extended straight back from its flat body, terminating in a thin, curved stinger. Night was descending and the scorpion was on the hunt. Cesar knew that this climbing scorpion, a bark scorpion, was especially poisonous. He also knew that it did not see well.

Voices in the next room crescendoed and now their words were clear. "How did you find my house?" Rosa asked.

Cesar's mother entertained a diverse array of suitors—shy men, bold men, gruff men, men of assorted ages, shapes and capacities. She was of medium build and pretty, with high cheekbones, long black hair, and quick dark eyes. She did not want for enthusiastic admirers, but they seldom visited more than once before fleeing her volcanic temper, which erupted as soon as they fell short of her uncertain expectations.

The man said, "How I found this place, you do not need to know." He is different, Cesar thought. He will not be moved.

"My son is nine and he is more of a man than you."

"I need a woman, not a child. Tonight you are going to be woman."

"You're drunk. Get out of my house."

The bark scorpion inched along the ceiling. Its hard exoskeletal legs scratched the rough cinderblock. Cesar whisked straight black hair away from his dark eyes and watched the scorpion move over his bed.

The boy formulated a plan: He would furl his discarded magazine into a club and vanquish the scorpion with a single blow. He knew he must not miss. The scorpion would pose an even greater threat if fell to the floor and hid.

"Get out of my house," Rosa said.

"Put that down."

Cesar heard furniture tumble and glass shatter. The bark scorpion froze and its stinger arched.

"Let me go," Rosa said.

"You asked for it." A slap sounded and Rosa shrieked.

The scorpion released from the wall and fell toward Cesar. He rolled off the bed and the scorpion landed behind him with a smack.

Cesar grabbed the magazine and twisted it into a tight baton, and swung the baton at a glancing angle that swept the scorpion onto the cement floor unharmed.

"Cesar, get Abuelito!" Rosa shouted.

The bark scorpion scurried toward the protective cover of the bed. Again the boy swung his paper club down. He reared back to strike another blow, but saw no scorpion.

Glued by its bodily fluids to Cesar's baton, the injured scorpion detached and dropped to the boy's bare shoulder and tumbled down his back, stinging wildly at the air. Cesar whirled around and saw the scorpion writhing on the floor. He smashed it again and again, and kneeled, panting, over the crumpled mass.

Rosa screamed. "Abuelito!" Her voice trailed away as she fled the house.

Cesar's bedroom door burst open and the boy sprang to his feet. The man standing in the doorway, Ramiro Ramos, was not tall, but his upper body was thick and his legs thin like a Brahma bull. Ginger whiskers and close-cropped hair framed his meaty, pale face, the rarest of complexions in the Baja. Ramos did his work at night.

"You must be the man of the house," Ramos said. He perspired and breathed fast, and his bloodshot eyes squinted through heavy lids.

Ramos saw Cesar's paper club and he raised his hands. "Look, I'm unarmed."

Cesar threw his magazine on the floor. "Now we're even."

Ramos grinned and advanced. "You and me are gonna teach your mama a lesson."

Cesar's grandfather, his *abuelito*, entered the front room clutching a long, thin fillet knife. "That's far enough," he said.

Ramos turned and regarded Abuelito through Cesar's open bedroom door. Abuelito wore a sparse silver beard and a tattered T-shirt hung on his thin frame. Abuelito's skin was earthen brown and his chin came to a point.

"Wait there, old man. I'll take care of you in a minute." Ramos looked at Cesar. "First you, kid."

Abuelito entered Cesar's bedroom. In a calm, steady voice, he said, "You must make a choice. I have made mine." He waved Ramos toward the front door with the filet knife.

Ramos smiled. "You are loco, old man. Your whole family is loco."

Abuelito locked eyes with Ramos. "Leave now." Ramos grinned and sidled around the knife. He feinted toward Abuelito and the tip of the knife rose to Ramos' chest.

Ramos tensed and lost his grin. He backed into the front room, never taking his eyes off Abuelito.

"This isn't done," he said. Ramos backed out the open front door and vanished into the night.

Abuelito walked to the front door and watched for a moment, then returned to Cesar's bedroom.

"You okay?"

The boy's hands trembled and his face was glossed with sweat. "Fine."

Rosa raced into Cesar's room. She knelt before her son and clutched his shoulders. "Did he hurt you?"

Cesar shook free of her grasp and looked away. "Why do you bring a man like that into our home?"

"I didn't bring him here. I don't know how he found this place."

"Well, he did, thanks to you."

"I will kill him if he touches you."

"Nobody's going to kill anyone," Abuelito said. "Let's all get some sleep. Or try."

Abuelito walked into the front room and righted a

topped chair. Without turning around, he said, "A recently-dead scorpion can be as dangerous as a living one. Take it away before you step on it. And lock the door." Abuelito left the house.

Cesar looked down. The lifeless bark scorpion lay between his and Rosa's bare feet. Abuelito sees everything, the boy thought.

2

In predawn darkness, Abuelito touched his grandson's bare shoulder. Cesar rolled out of bed and slid his feet into his sandals. He tugged on a T-shirt and followed his grandfather into the front room.

A small lamp lit the modest space. A single square window, the same size as Cesar's bedroom window, admitted little light at any hour.

The room was outfitted with a cabinet, small counter and sink, two-burner electric hotplate, bookcase with no books, and square table surrounded by four mismatching chairs. Yellowed clear plastic overlaid a pear-and-plum-motif tablecloth. In the center of the table a bouquet of pink plastic roses in a chipped faux crystal glass vase stood between glass Eifel Tower salt and pepper shakers. A mournful ballad of lost love droned from a portable radio on top of a small white refrigerator.

Rosa stood at the counter and placed two burritos in a brown paper sack. She wore a powder-blue maid's uniform and her hair was coiled in a bun.

Rosa handed the sack to Cesar. "Save the bag," she said. "I'll use it again."

A horn tooted outside. Rosa stuffed a third burrito in another sack and carried it out the open front door.

Cesar and Abuelito trailed Rosa into the faint early morning light. They watched her enter the backseat door of a dilapidated station wagon and join three women who wore the same powder-blue uniforms. Rosa rolled down the window and waved as the station wagon pulled away.

Abuelito's squeaky VW bus ground in and out of first and second gears as it trundled along a winding dirt road between slate gray hills. The bus's dim headlights lit the rutted road five feet ahead. Cesar sat next to Abuelito in the front seat and clung to a ceiling handle as the timeworn vehicle lurched and pitched. The bus arrived at the paved two-lane coast road and turned north, and Cesar released his grip.

"Would you have used the knife?" Cesar asked.

"If someone intended to harm you or your mama, I would use it without hesitation. It would be my duty."

Cesar had heard Abuelito discuss *duty* before. The old man only invoked the word in matters of greatest importance. Two years earlier a powerful hurricane grazed the coast and threatened to tear away their house's tarp-and-metal roof, which terrified and delighted the boy beyond measure. Mud and rock washed down from the hills above the village and backed up against homes and cars, and knocked down just about everything else in its path before it slopped over the road and spilled into the sea. Abuelito defended the roof for two days and two nights in howling wind and hammering rain. Lives were lost during the tempest, but the old man never shrank from its fierce assault. Abuelito explained to Cesar that it was his duty.

"He is bigger and stronger than you."

"I would also have an advantage. When a man commits fully to a thing he cannot be stopped."

"Why would mama take up with someone like him?"

"The lonely heart is a complicated."

"She has us."

"Your mama works at the hotel six days a week. She is tired. She is lonely. She takes her chances."

"Is it worth it?"

"Sometimes, no."

A southbound school bus whooshed by and rocked the VW bus. Cesar thought about the students who waited for the bus each morning by the side of the coast road. The girls were dressed in white blouses, plaid skirts and shiny black shoes; the boys wore white shirts, gray slacks and scuffed shoes. Cesar could not understand why they would choose to spend their days in school and he prayed that they did not despair their fates. He was happy with his sandals, T-shirts and patched jeans, and whiling his days on the ocean with his grandfather. He looked forward to a life on the sea—especially the day when he would catch his blue marlin.

The VW bus pulled into a long, narrow parking lot that extended between a small harbor and row of ramshackle restaurants. Lights were already on inside the buildings as staff prepared for the morning rush. Low sand dunes marked the western boundary of the harbor, which opened to the sea between parallel rock jetties.

Sport fishing boats with white fiberglass hulls and blue canvas canopies were tied up to the docks closest to the harbor mouth. Cesar referred to them as *white boats* ever since his first visit to the harbor. The boy revered the white boats and their preeminent position in the harbor's nautical hierarchy, and he always thrilled at their sight. The white boats embodied everything Cesar wanted and everything he did not have. He planned to crew on a white boat when he was older, as had his grandfather when he was young.

Abuelito parked the VW bus at the end of the parking lot, where the smallest craft tethered to a dilapidated wooden dock, and turned off the headlights. He stepped out of the bus and slid the side cargo door open. Inside, four 5-gallon plastic buckets, assorted fishing tackle, rope, rags and a long-handled fish net lay a heap.

Abuelito gathered the buckets and two light fishing rods, set them on the ground. He placed fishing tackle and the brown paper bag that held the burritos in one bucket. Only an occasional squawk from a restless seagull broke the early-morning calm.

"Don't forget—"

"The net," Cesar said. The boy shook the fish net free from the heap inside the bus. Abuelito shut the door and they tromped down the narrow springy dock. A cluster of small craft, none recent, wedged together on both sides.

Abuelito stopped in front of a 12-foot wooden skiff, red with blue trim, and slippery with dew. Plastic fenders hung off the sides of larger boats in the harbor, but not the skiff, which had achieved a hardened immunity to further damage after decades of rugged service.

The old man set the buckets and fishing rods on the dock, then pulled a rope tie to bring the skiff close. Cesar boarded first, sidestepping two splintery wooden oars that lay on the floor. He laid the fish net down and sopped dew off the benches with a rag, and sat on the middle bench.

Abuelito handed the rods and buckets to the boy, untied the skiff, and stepped into the boat. He sat on the rear bench and swirled a red gas can to measure its contents, then tilted the propeller of a tarnished Evinrude outboard motor down into the water. He squeezed the Evinrude's primer bulb and yanked the pull cord, and the motor sputtered to life.

Abuelito grasped the tiller and backed the skiff out of its place in the line of boats, then guided it through the harbor past the white boats and entered the open sea.

3

The ocean was placid and a hue deeper than the indigo sky. The skiff motored north and Cesar gazed up at the stars, finding familiar arrangements that expressed forms and figures known only to him.

With no prompting from his grandfather the boy picked up a fishing rod and unhooked a snap swivel that secured the end of the line to a guide. He unrolled a rigging from a plastic spool—four feathered jigs on a three-foot leader—and connected it to the line.

Cesar and Abuelito's preparations followed a similar routine; only the baitfish that they sought changed. Sometimes they fished for green jack, distinguished by dull white underbellies and light green vertical bars. When sardines were running, Abuelito's silvery jigs might bring in several at a time. Flying fish were elusive, but always valued bait stock. In recent weeks caballitos, with large eyes and forked tails, had been hitting the feathered jigs hard. All of the baitfish were esteemed by captains of the white boats for their appeal to big game fish—sailfish, tuna, dorado, yellowtail, white seabass, roosterfish, and especially marlin.

Abuelito knew how to catch the baitfish and he knew how to sell them. Today Cesar and his grandfather would travel one mile out of the harbor and five miles up the coast, fill their buckets with caballitos, and motor back in time to intercept white boats laden with American tourists as they left the harbor. The captains relied on Abuelito for fresh, live baitfish and he always delivered. Years earlier he learned that the captains would find other sources for live bait if he missed even a single day and he never disappointed them again.

The white boats travelled far offshore to chase the most prized of the billfish—blue, white and black marlin. Cesar was proud that a caballito that his grandfather reeled in might entice a trophy marlin. One day he would tempt a blue marlin with his own baitfish.

Abuelito scanned the glassy water and cut the engine. The boat's momentum carried it forward a short distance before it surrendered to the ocean's undulate grasp. The hushed break of small early morning waves on the shore carried across the silky surface to the skiff.

Cesar handed the fishing rod to Abuelito and filled the buckets with seawater. Abuelito cast his line and the rig broke the glassy surface with a delicate plop. He raised and dipped his rod to release line from the openface reel as the feathered jigs sank.

When the rig reached depth, Abuelito cranked the reel and fluttered his fishing rod to make the jigs dance. Cesar watched the rod against the dark sky. The tip trembled and Abuelito jerked the rod back. The line went taut and the rod bowed. Abuelito brought a caballito close to the skiff and Cesar wet his hands in the ocean. In the low light the ten-inch fish emitted a ghostly shimmer.

Abuelito raised the wriggling caballito out of the water and swung it toward Cesar. The boy closed his hands around the fish and lowered it into a bucket. He removed the hook and covered the bucket with a wet rag to prevent the vigorous fish from escaping. Abuelito cast again and brought in another caballito moments later.

"The ocean is good to us today," he said. "Of course, the ocean is always good."

Every time Abuelito cast his line a caballito struck, and he reeled in fish after fish. Cesar removed the hooks and deposited the caballitos in the buckets as fast as they came over the side of the boat. Before the sun rose over the hills to the east, all four buckets were full with frisky baitfish.

"Let's eat," Abuelito said.

Cesar and his grandfather ate their burritos and the only sounds they heard were the gurgle of water under the skiff and break of far-off waves. Onshore, vehicles' headlights flashed along the coast road. Above the road, lights inside resort hotels that climbed the hills began to flicker on. Many of the hotels were designed in a style indigenous to the region, with stucco arches and adobe roof tiles. Abuelito viewed the buildings as another sort of bait, aimed at luring affluent tourists.

"You always know where to find the baitfish," Cesar said. "And you always know what they're biting."

"Not always."

"Look—four full buckets. Every day, four full buckets."

"It takes many years to know the fish. And then you learn that you will never truly know them."

"Tell me about the caballitos."

"I have told you about caballitos."

"One more time, in case I missed something."

Abuelito was pleased that his grandson was eager to learn the ways of the fish and he was glad to share his knowledge. "Caballitos come up from deep water after the sun sets and they use their big round eyes to find food. They like warm water; you will not find them much further north. If the water is quiet and the skies are clear, caballitos will chase the feathered jigs with a passion, as they did today. Marlin may be tempted by many baitfish, but they cannot resist a caballito."

Cesar committed Abuelito's words to memory, as he did whenever his grandfather shared bits of wisdom that might help him catch a blue marlin.

The sun had cleared the hills by the time Cesar and Abuelito motored back down the coast. A gentle breeze brushed glimmering ripples across the awakening sea. Curtains opened in the hotel rooms and vehicles drove the coast road with headlights off. Abuelito wore a weathered white cap, the bill tipped toward the sun, and Cesar tied a rag around the top of his head for protection.

Along the way, Cesar dipped the fishing net in the water and scooped up plastic bottles and bags, foam sandals, Styrofoam containers, and all manner of plastic debris, and dumped it on the floor of the boat. "On your left, Cesar," Abuelito said, guiding the skiff toward a new target. "To your right." Some of the debris was labeled with exotic markings that absorbed the boy's imagination.

The previous week, Cesar spotted a seagull standing on a floating mass, tearing away bits of food with its sharp yellow beak. Abuelito steered a course for the mass and stood as the skiff drew near. He eyed the mass and gunned the Evinrude, veering away and tumbling his startled grandson to the floor of the boat. The seagull took flight and abandoned its meal, but circled back to its perch after the skiff pulled away. "It is not your Abuelito's ocean," the old man said, and he did not speak of the matter again.

Abuelito guided the skiff between the jetties and into the harbor. Cesar wound the rig with the feathered jigs around the plastic spool. Caballitos splashed in the buckets.

Inboard motors rumbled as white boats pulled away from the docks and started toward the harbor mouth. Abuelito jockeyed the skiff close to the procession and cut the engine.

A captain puffed a cigar on the fly bridge of a passing white boat. "Should of got here earlier, amigo," he called. "Already got our bait."

Abuelito smiled and waved. "Good luck."

Another white boat passed, then another. Abuelito smiled and waved at each passing boat.

The next white boat slowed. "What do you have for us?" the captain asked. He wore a crisp white cap with a nautical insignia.

Abuelito raised a squirming fish from a bucket. "Caballitos."

"Scad, huh?"

"You catch big marlin with these."

The captain conferred with a crewman. "How much for a bucket?" the crewman asked.

"Thirty-five dollars," Abuelito said. "Many fish."

"Twenty-five sounds better."

"Thirty-five," Cesar said. Abuelito glanced at Cesar and frowned.

"Twenty-five," the captain said. "Our best offer."

"Good, good," Abuelito said. "Twenty-five."

The crewman extended a long pole to Abuelito. He grabbed the pole and pulled the skiff alongside the white boat. Cesar hoisted a bucket. The crewman took the handle and brought the bucket aboard, and poured the caballitos into a live bait well. He tossed the empty bucket back to Cesar and paid Abuelito.

After they sold their baitfish, Cesar and Abuelito would fill their empty buckets with the plastic debris that they collected on their return trip to the harbor and deposit the trash in 55-gallon steel drums at the end of the parking lot. Sometimes they climbed over the sand dunes and gathered more plastic debris on the beach, of which there was an unending supply, and contributed it to the drums. The trash was hauled away by municipal workers at irregular intervals and the drums often spilled over. Abuelito once brought several empty drums that he found in a field to the harbor to address the surplus, but they soon overflowed, too.

A couple years earlier, two university students—a petite girl with long, straight hair and attentive eyes, and a tall, gangly boy with curly hair and a warm smile—visited the harbor. The students arrayed a folding table with literature that warned of the dangers of plastic pollution. They told Cesar and Abuelito about a giant island of plastic in the middle of the ocean, and the threat that it posed to fish and wildlife, and even people. Cesar and Abuelito admired the students' passion for protecting the ocean they so loved, and they accepted every piece of literature the students offered, even though they could not read a word of it. They pledged to do their best to curb further damage to a natural resource that had provided for their family for generations.

For a time, Cesar thought he would like to attend the university and tell fishermen about the great plastic island, but he knew his future was on the white boats. Cesar would be able to catch marlin and protect the ocean without burdening himself with the unnecessary distraction of school.

4

I n the parking lot, Abuelito closed the VW bus's cargo door and watched a creaky wooden boat dock near the skiff. The words "El Bucanero" were painted in crude orange script on the boat's peeling green hull. The small wheelhouse was a mottled yellow with white trim.

Abuelito climbed into the front seat of the bus next to Cesar and said, "We sold many fish, but we did not account for our dinner. Maybe Miguel brought in some tuna." He handed several bills to his grandson.

"Me?"

Abuelito rested his arms on the steering wheel and gazed out the front window. "If you can catch a fish, you can eat. But sometimes you must buy a fish to eat."

Cesar stared at the bills in his hand, more money than he had ever held in his life.

"Bargain well," Abuelito said. "Miguel is a shark."

Miguel and his son Guillermo secured the El Bucanero to the dock as Cesar approached. Their jeans were stiff with dry fish blood and guts, and an acrid stench of guano clung to the boat.

Miguel's face was soft and round, unlike any shark the boy had ever seen. Guillermo, a smaller, pudgier version of his father, smirked when he saw Cesar.

Miguel said, "They were biting today, Cesar. Did you catch many fish?"

Sensing an opening, Guillermo asked, "Or did you catch more buckets of garbage?"

"We filled our buckets with caballitos and sold them all," Cesar said.

"We had a good day, too." Miguel opened a waist-high metal cooler on the rear deck and pulled out a blunt-headed dorado that stretched from his shoulder to his feet. Squawking seagulls converged from all directions and hovered over the boat like scraps of white paper in a whirlwind.

"That's a big dorado," Cesar said. "One of the biggest I have seen."

"Almost as big as you, but stronger," Miguel said. He laid the Dorado back in the cooler and slammed the lid closed, silencing the birds. "The biggest dorado are as smart as they are strong. That is how they got so big, no?"

"One of these times you should show us a fish you caught," Guillermo said. "Just so we'll know you wasn't lying."

"Do you have any tuna to sell?" Cesar asked Miguel.

"Some excellent albacore. Come look."

Cesar stepped onto the rear deck and Miguel cracked the cooler. Cesar peered inside and saw a dozen albacore tuna, each fish not less than ten pounds, lying beside the dorado on a half-melted bed of ice.

"Each one a meal," Miguel said.

The seagulls resumed circling and squawking.

"How much for one?"

"Ten. Fifteen for two."

One side of Guillermo's mouth curled in a grin. The other side frowned. "Can you afford it?"

"Hush, Gui. I'm conducting business."

Cesar turned and saw Abuelito sitting motionless in the VW bus, staring straight ahead.

"I'm sure they are fair prices," Cesar said.

"Fair prices? They are the best prices you will find."

"We can only spend five dollars."

"I must feed my family too, Cesar. Seven."

Cesar's eyes sharpened. "Six."

"Six?" Guillermo protested.

"And I choose the fish. My best offer."

Miguel gazed into Cesar's eyes and measured his resolve, then laughed and shook the boy's hand. "Just like your grandfather. When you make up your mind there is no changing it. This time, six. But just this time. Take the fattest, juiciest albacore you can find."

Guillermo glared at his father. "Papa!"

"Do something useful," Miguel said. Guillermo threw a menacing look at Cesar and ducked into the cabin.

Cesar handed Miguel six dollars and selected a tuna, and Miguel wrapped it in newspaper.

Cesar walked down the dock and glanced back at the El Bucanero. Guillermo waved his fist and mouthed some unbearable oath through the cracked cabin door window.

Cesar climbed into the front seat of the VW bus. He unwrapped the newspaper and displayed the tuna for his grandfather, who continued to stare out the front window. "Six dollars," the boy said, exalting in his triumphant negotiation. Abuelito started the bus and Cesar rewrapped the fish. The engine idled and the bus remained stationary.

Cesar's victorious moment was fading fast. "Are we going?"

"Trash."

Cesar set the fish down and stepped out the door. He dashed to the front of the bus where the four trash-filled buckets rested. He toted them to the 55-gallon drums and dumped their contents, and raced back to the bus, the empty buckets swinging at his sides. He flung the buckets into the back of the bus rejoined his grandfather.

Abuelito looked at his grandson and smiled. "You did well, Cesar." The boy glowed with pride as the bus pulled away.

5

A long train of cars, trucks and service vehicles formed behind the VW bus as it poked south on the coast road. The vehicles sped around the VW when there was an opening in the northbound lane and honked, but the bus did not move any faster.

Abuelito swung the bus across the road and drove beneath a beige stucco arch onto an immaculate blacktop driveway, lined with evenly-spaced cacti and uplights, that curved up a hillside. Adjacent to the arch, a stucco sign with raised lettering read "Posada De Tortugas." A bas relief of a lime green sea turtle angled toward the letters.

"Where are we going?" Cesar asked.

"A place I remember well."

At the top of the driveway the bus pulled into the drive-through entrance of the hotel and stopped. Stucco arches similar to the one by the coast road rimmed the overhang and bore the same raised lettering and bas relief sea turtles.

A bronze-skinned valet wearing khaki shorts and a white polo shirt with an embroidered Posada De Tortugas logo appeared at Abuelito's open window. "The service entrance is around back," he said.

"I would like to show my grandson the property. We won't stay long."

"Do you have business with the hotel?"

"I stayed here once."

"There are parking spaces around the side." The valet leaned close and spoke in a low voice. "Security might hassle you."

"Thank you, my friend."

Abuelito drove the bus around the corner of the hotel and parked. He and Cesar walked to a low stone wall high above the coast road. A warm breeze carried the sweet fragrance of dry grasses up the hillside. A yellow convertible Mustang curled down the black driveway and turned south on the coast road. Beyond, a line of brown pelicans flew low along the shore.

"You stayed here?" Cesar asked.

"I was not much older than you when my papa went to California. He found work in the lettuce fields and sent us money. It was a great help for we had no other means. His letters became fewer and eventually the money stopped. In his last letter he said the lettuce ran out and he would need to find a new crop. It was hard for my mother, but she kept faith. She could not find work—there were no hotels here then—and it was a losing battle. For a time, we survived on the fish that I caught, but it was not enough. One day I came home and my mother and sister were gone. She told a neighbor that she would send for me as soon she could. I was on my own. I had to take care of myself."

"What did you do?"

"I resolved to find my father and reunite my family. I packed a small bag and started walking north. Some older boys confronted me and took my sandals. They were all I had but the boys had to steal something. They left me bleeding on the ground—just down there—and said they would finish the job if they saw me again." Abuelito hooked a finger in his mouth and pulled back his right cheek, revealing a gap in his upper teeth. "My encounter with those boys has made for much unrequited work by those unfortunate teeth on the other side."

Cesar stared at the coast road and imagined his grandfather as a boy lying by the side of the road, bleeding and alone. He swished his tongue over his teeth.

"I took refuge here, on this very spot. Nature owned this place then."

Cesar glanced around the grounds and imagined the hill before the hotel came.

"I sat here and watched the sea for several days. The warm breeze, the aromas, the light—they are still familiar. I had nothing to eat and I became weak. Then the sea spoke to me, as clearly as I am speaking you now. The sea told me that I should not worry, that she would provide. I was afraid, and yet I was never more certain that things would be alright. Ever since, the sea has provided, just as she promised those many years ago. A good thing, too. For a while, the coyotes sang to me. Then they stopped singing and announced their intention to eat me. That was when I left this place and returned home."

"Did you see your mama and papa again?"

A beefy security guard wearing a black uniform and black wraparound sunglasses approached at a brisk pace. He tilted his head toward his shoulder and spoke into a tiny device.

"You have business with the hotel?" the security guard asked.

"No," Abuelito said.

"Guests?"

"No."

"Then you got to go. This is private property."

The security guard talked into his shoulder as Cesar and Abuelito drove away.

The VW bus turned off the coast road and lurched along a one-lane dirt road that snaked through brown hills blotched with low brush and cacti. The bus cleared the hills and puttered over a rise, and descended into the remains of a tiny fishing village, sustained now by a dribble of water and electricity that an ambitious resort developer brought through the hills before he abandoned all further efforts to tame the remote place. The village stretched along a sloping strip of land between the hills and sea that fell off at a low crumbling cliff by the water's edge.

A roadrunner dashed in front of the VW bus as it passed a tumbledown adobe hut that the villagers scrupulously avoided. Twisted, riven driftwood rafters and beams jutted from the rubble at odd angles, goading the villagers' unease that the hut was in the malign grip of some sinister invisible force.

The bus puttered by several well-spaced cinderblock

houses topped with plywood and corrugated metal roofs. Further along, two naked toddlers sat on a weather-beaten sofa spooning rice out of bowls in front of a decaying RV that rested on blocks. Behind the RV, laundry swayed on ropes strung between driftwood posts at opposite ends of an infilled yard braced by stacked bald tires. Across the road, six ribbed fingers of a cardón cactus reached skyward. Cesar secretly watched the cardón whenever the bus passed, but he never caught the fingers moving.

Few objects started life new in the village, but they usually lived longer. Several abandoned structures—some half-built, some crumbling, all uninhabitable—provided replacement parts for the other dwellings. Half of the homes had cisterns of a sort, mostly repurposed plastic and steel barrels that caught winter rainwater that ran off the roofs. On the hillside, a corroding steel water tank that Abuelito rigged up decades earlier still provided for some of his family's needs.

The village offered no stores, businesses, services, schools, cell towers, doctors, or help when needed—only isolation and privation. The residents depended on the abject bleakness of the place to discourage further encroachments by those who might disrupt their tenuous, but treasured solitude.

At the south end of the village the VW bus circled a turnaround on a flat bluff that rose twenty feet above a potbellied cove. A shallow, soft-yellow beach curved along the back of the cove and could be accessed by a steep path that angled down a lumpy wall of dirt, stone and brush. At the bottom of the wall, piles of small boulders formed a natural riprap erosion barrier.

The water in the cove was crystalline close to shore. Ripples in the sloping yellow sand were still visible toward the middle of the cove, where the sand disappeared under emerald green water that transitioned again to a deep, luminous blue.

The VW bus stopped in front of Cesar and Abuelito's house. A dense bougainvillea grew up one side of the gray concrete structure and arched over the front door, creating a natural arbor. Its papery crimson bracts held the sunlight and glowed. Abuelito groomed and trained the bougainvillea like a cherished pet, maintaining its luster with a steady diet of dishwater and fish scraps. The house's front door was open, as it usually was when the family was home, as much to allow daylight as fresh air.

Annexed to the house was a tarpaper-clad plywood structure. A blue plastic tarp, fastened with tacked lath, served as a roof.

Across the road, Señora Muñoz and her middle-aged daughter, Fatima, sat in the narrow shade in front of their cinderblock house. They wore bright, colorful shawls and loose cotton dresses, and their long thick hair was parted down the middle and tied back. Señora Muñoz's face was brown and furrowed like the hills above the village. Like other village residents, the Muñoz women kept to themselves. Cesar never once saw them on his side of the road.

In the afternoons, the Muñoz women crafted colorful Huichol yarn paintings on boards that rested on their laps. The yarn paintings' intricate motifs of nature, birds, animals, corn and peyote expressed the Huichol people's belief in a sacred relationship between people and nature.

Once each week, a blonde sales agent who favored tan pantsuits pulled up in a shiny SUV to pick up the Muñoz women's newest yarn paintings, which she sold to gift shops and art galleries. The sales agent kept the women well-stocked in plastic fiber—polyester, nylon and acrylic—delivering skeins of synthetic yarn with each visit. The brightly-colored yarn paintings sold well; tourists were eager to acquire examples of authentic Mexican culture. Had the sales agent asked, the Muñoz women might have shared that they were themselves of the Huichol people, and that their yarn paintings, destined to hang in tourists' living rooms and offices and dens, whispered wisdom of the ancients. The sales agent never asked.

"Good day, señoras," Abuelito said. "Cesar, take half of the tuna to Señora Muñoz."

Abuelito entered the plywood annex through a hatch. Cesar opened the cargo door and gathered the fishing gear, and followed Abuelito inside. The blue tarp roof lay atop spans of rope and crackled when the hatch opened and closed. Fresh air entered through two screened vents.

During the daytime, the tarp cast a diffuse blue glow. Cesar liked to imagine that he was entering a magical undersea realm when he stepped inside. He set the fishing rods, buckets and net in a corner, and placed the spooled rig on a shelf in a bookcase that held reserves of canned food and sacks of beans and rice. A small round table and two chairs stood on the plywood floor in a corner of the annex. A sarape lay atop a deteriorating foam rubber matt on a platform bed similar to Cesar's. An upturned plastic crate served as a bedside table. Deep sea fishing magazines leaned inside the crate. On top, literature given to Cesar and Abuelito by the university students was organized in a neat stack.

Above Abuelito's bed a dusty deep sea fishing rod with a corroded chrome Penn reel rested on two nails. Monofilament line threaded through the guides to the tip of the rod and attached to a metal leader. At the end of the leader a large J-hook dug into the rod's pocked rubber grip.

Cesar kneeled on the bed and inspected the deep sea rod. "Did you catch blue marlin with this?"

"Many blue marlin, as I have told you many times."

"When will I catch mine?"

"When you are ten."

Cesar looked at Abuelito. "Ten? I'm almost ten."

"That's right."

The boy's eyes glowed. "Really?"

Abuelito nodded and smiled. "Really."

Cesar leaped off the bed and hugged his grandfather tight.

"We will need a boat that can chase the biggest blue marlin far out to sea," Abuelito said. "We will need a white boat."

Hope drained from the boy. "We don't have a white boat."

"When you are ten I will buy a day for us on a white boat. I have saved the money. You will catch your blue marlin, and I will be there to see it."

Cesar hugged his grandfather again. The boy wondered at the transformative power of aging and prayed his years would come fast.

Each day during the next week Cesar and Abuelito journeyed to the harbor before dawn. The caballitos were running and the fishermen quickly filled their buckets. When they returned to the harbor, Abuelito directed the skiff toward floating plastic debris and Cesar netted the trash.

One morning Abuelito steered the skiff toward a long, flat object that bobbed high on the water. Cesar pulled in a 10-foot blue plastic longboard that probably floated away from one of the resorts. The longboard's skeg was missing and one edge bore a deep dent.

"Maybe you can use it in the cove," Abuelito said.

In the corner of Cesar's bedroom, cardboard boxes overflowed with sporting goods retrieved from the sea—soccer balls, volleyballs, basketballs, baseballs and baseball bats, footballs, tennis balls, Frisbees, a tennis racket and a hockey stick. Surfing would not require a court or field or gym or even another player, all of which the boy lacked. With the longboard, he would only need some waves.

After Cesar and his grandfather returned home, Abuelito laid a piece of plywood on the ground in front of his annex and set the plastic longboard on the plywood. He ringed the dent with cardboard and lined the cardboard with aluminum foil, and directed the sun's reflection at the dent. After awhile the dented plastic became soft to the touch. Abuelito removed the foil ring and laid a plank over the dent, and drove a front tire of his VW bus on top of the plank. That evening, Abuelito backed his bus off the plank and the dent was almost entirely gone.

Abuelito fashioned a skeg from a piece of a salvaged plastic pallet and affixed it to the longboard, and Cesar was good to go.

Rosa scraped a mound of minced onions off a cutting board into a pot of beans that bubbled on the hotplate. On the other burner, half of the albacore tuna sizzled in a pan. Chopped cabbage and a stack of tortillas waited on another board, and an open jar of homemade salsa was close at hand.

Cesar sat at the dining table and watched Abuelito screw two rusty latches, spaced several feet apart, to the front door.

"Go outside for a moment," Abuelito said. Cesar went outside. Abuelito closed the door and pushed half-bent 16-penny nails through the latches.

"Open the door," Abuelito said.

Cesar pushed and yanked the door handle.

"Harder."

Cesar spread his feet and put his full weight into the effort. The door remained shut. Abuelito said to Rosa, "Nobody's getting through this door unless you choose to let them in."

Abuelito removed the nails. He admitted Cesar and clapped the boy on the shoulder. "Cesar! Where have you been? We missed you."

The next Sunday Cesar and Abuelito took showers

under a garden hose hanging from a hook behind the house and Rosa trimmed their hair. The family donned its Sunday best and travelled inland to the old pueblo of Rio Seco.

They prayed in the pueblo's whitewashed Spanish chapel and strolled to the bustling central plaza where mariachis performed, revelers danced, and chaste young couples promenaded around a tall colonial fountain. Water trickled from the fountain's three cascading bowls into a broad basin girded by a terra cotta tile bench, where Cesar and Abuelito sat and watched the merriment.

Occasional fireworks flashed and popped and the air was heavy with aromas of spice and gunpowder. On the periphery of the plaza, somber young men sought the attention of pretty señoritas who feigned ignorance of their longing gazes. Street vendors dispensed tacos, huaraches, tortas, tamales, sopes and quesadillas from pushcarts and pop-up taquerias. Tourists in T-shirts bearing logos of dive shops, sport fishing charters, cantinas and coastal hotspots pursued authentic experiences through the lenses of their smartphone cameras.

Toward dark, the roars of men in a side alley reverberated off adobe and stone walls. The men had gathered to watch contestants square off in bare-knuckle fistfights, a long tradition in Rio Seco. The contestants vied for the respect of their peers, honor of their families, and muscular reputations that would be known in distant pueblos. More than once Cesar begged Abuelito to take him to see the fights, but his grandfather said, "There is enough violence. We don't need to seek it out."

They watched Rosa dance with a succession of eager partners. She teamed with a handsome man dressed in a shimmery white shirt and black slacks. Rosa and the man matched steps like practiced professionals and the crowd moved back to admire their skillful footwork.

Abuelito watched Rosa and said to Cesar, "Your mama is beautiful and talented. You should be proud to be her son."

At the end of the dance the handsome man dipped Rosa and her hair brushed the tiled plaza. He whisked her to her feet and bowed low. Onlookers applauded, and Rosa beamed and nodded acknowledgement.

A well-pregnant woman pushed through the crowd and entwined her arms around the handsome man's neck, and Rosa saw matching gold bands on their ring fingers. She frowned and turned away, and strode to Cesar and Abuelito. "Ready?"

"It's early," Cesar said.

"We haven't eaten," Abuelito said.

"I don't know why I don't come alone," Rosa said with a grimace. "I don't know why I do anything I do." She grabbed her purse and marched away.

"Your mama needs to catch her breath," Abuelito said. "I will find something tasty to eat. Wait here."

Cesar watched Abuelito wend his way through swirling dancers and fold into the crowd. The sun dipped behind buildings on the western edge of the plaza and cast a long shadow that crept past the fountain. Strings of paper lantern and chili pepper lights flickered on.

The shouts of men watching the fights in the alley overcame a six-piece mariachi band's most vigorous efforts and, finally, Cesar's willpower. The boy peered through the crowd toward the alley, and then stood on the bench and strained to catch a glimpse of the action. He turned and looked for his grandfather, but saw only the whirling revelers.

Cesar stepped off the bench and moved to the opposite side of the fountain, and made his way toward the alley.

6

Cesar cleared the plaza and entered the dank passageway. Ahead, men crowded wall to wall and exhorted combatants. "Jab him! Left hand, left hand! Lower—in the gut!"

For a moment the men's shouts abated. A dull thud punctuated the lull, followed by a deafening cheer. Arms speared the air and shouts of "olé" volleyed through the alley, signifying the end of the bout.

The mob slacked and Cesar squirmed his way to the center of the human arena, which reeked of smoke and sweat. Spectators' eyes receded below their brows under the glare of high wall lights.

Cesar saw two men lead the defeated fighter away. His arms draped over his seconds' shoulders for support. The victorious fighter followed and offered words of encouragement to his vanquished opponent. The combatants were friendly competitors who fought only for bragging rights.

A squat middle-aged man wearing studded black cowboy boots, black jeans, and an oversized black cowboy hat with a silver band stepped forward. "And now for our main fight," he said. "You all know our reigning champion—Alejandro Rodriguez, the Jalisco Hurricane."

A new fighter—tall, shirtless, and already wearing a light sheen of sweat—skipped into the ring and shadow-boxed. A red bandana was tied around his forehead.

The crowd cheered and applauded. The champ pumped his bare fist in the air.

The man in the black cowboy hat continued. "To-night we have a new challenger who fought here for just the first time last month. If you were here, you saw our newcomer do things we have never before witnessed. Think twice before you bet against him. Let's meet our challenger."

The crowd awaited the second fighter's entrance. Af-ter several minutes, the champ stopped shadowboxing and chatted with some in the crowd. "Let's go!" a specta-tor shouted. "Time to fight!"

Several in the crowd booed. "Show your face!" one bellowed.

Opposite Cesar, spectators were jostled and shoved aside as the challenger pushed his way toward the ring. The mob pressed forward and tightened like a noose, locking Cesar into the front row of spectators. The chal-lenger stepped into the ring and was greeted by the big-gest roar of the night. Apprehension gripped the boy. The Jalisco's Hurricane's opponent was Ramiro Ramos.

Ramos clutched a half-empty bottle of tequila. He took a long swig and handed the bottle to a spectator. Ramos wore a tight T-shirt and his bulging biceps were only slightly thicker than his massive forearms. He tugged his T-shirt over his head, revealing a thick, pale trunk stacked with horizontal bands of muscle. Ramos raised his fists and turned slowly, and locked his eyes on the champ.

The Jalisco Hurricane pranced forward and tapped fists with Ramos. The fighters drew back and a chant went up. "Fight! Fight! Fight!"

The man in the black cowboy hat raised his hand high and chopped the air. "Fight!"

The fighters cocked their arms and circled the ring, taking each other's measure. The champ danced forward and landed two quick left-hand jabs to Ramos' face. The mob shouted its approval. Ramos wiped his forearm over his mouth. Blood streaked his pale skin. Ramos smiled and his teeth glistened pink. He lowered his arms and leaned toward the champ, making no effort to dodge stinging jabs that found their target again and again, reddening Ramos' face with blood. Still he threw no punches.

The bloody spectacle immobilized Cesar with fascination and revulsion. Behind him, a spectator said, "It's coming. Any moment now."

The Jalisco Hurricane jabbed with his left hand and threw a looping right. For the first time, Ramos ducked the punch and launched a sweeping left hook into the champ's unguarded ribcage, lifting him off the alley floor.

The champ slumped to his knees and clutched his chest, moaning and gasping for air. The crowd thundered its approval: "Olé! Olé!" Ramos retrieved his bottle of tequila and took a swig, and sauntered toward his kneeling adversary.

"Finish him," a spectator said.

Ramos took another swig and stepped into a round-house uppercut that exploded the champ's nose and knocked him out cold. The mob groaned at Ramos' wanton brutality, a flagrant breach of the fights' time-honored code of conduct.

Ramos clutched the neck of the empty tequila bottle and smashed it on the alley floor. He raised the broken bottle high in the air like a trophy and paced the edge of the ring. Cesar wriggled backwards as Ramos drew near, but the mob convulsed and pushed the boy directly into his path.

Ramos saw Cesar and grinned. The boy backpedaled against the wall of spectators. Ramos seized a handful of Cesar's shirt and lifted him off the ground with one hand. A savage gleam appeared in his eyes. "Good to see you, kid."

A shrill whistle echoed off the walls and someone shouted, "Police!" The mob stampeded toward both ends of the alley, uncertain of the whistle's direction.

Ramos raised the jagged bottle to Cesar's eye and twisted it like the dial of a combination lock. "My gift to your mama."

Wrinkled brown fingers enlaced around Ramos' neck and jerked him backward. Ramos grunted and his eyes went wide. He released Cesar's shirt and the boy fell to the alley floor.

Ramos wheeled and scooped the broken bottle into the unseen figure, and his hand was empty when he drew it back. Ramos turned to Cesar and smiled a pink smile, then dashed away as federal police converged.

Cesar saw Abuelito lying on the ground next to three tacos, their contents splattered across the alley. The old man's bloody hands clutched the neck of the broken bottle, now impaled in his abdomen. His stricken eyes softened when he saw his grandson.

Cesar cradled his grandfather's head. "I'm sorry, Abuelito, I'm sorry." Tears streamed down the boy's cheeks.

Abuelito clutched Cesar's arm. "I love you, grandson. I will always be near," he said, and life went out of his eyes.

Word of violence swept through the plaza like a brush fire. Within minutes the music stopped, dancers dispersed, and vendors packed and departed. The strings of paper lantern and chili pepper lights swayed silently in a light breeze.

During the commotion, Rosa circled the fountain in search of her son and father. She followed federal police into the alley and saw the Jalisco Hurricane being rolled out on a stretcher. For a moment she breathed a sigh of relief that the violence did not concern Cesar or Abuelito. Then she saw a cluster of federal police and onlookers standing over a prone figure and speaking in hushed tones. In the middle of the group she glimpsed Cesar crouching over Abuelito.

Rosa pushed her way toward them, but an officer pulled her away.

"My father! My son!"

"The man is your father?"

"Let me go!"

The officer held Rosa's arms. "Señora, your father was stabbed."

"Let go of me! I need to see him!"

"I am sorry, señora. You can do nothing for him. He is dead."

Rosa collapsed to her knees and emitted a keening wail that blew through the alley like an icy wind.

7

The sun was high overhead when a dusty federal police car pulled up to Cesar's house the next day. Two officers stepped out of the car—paunchy and graying Jose Ruiz and decades-younger Alejandro Diaz, wiry and bent like a loaded spring. Each shoulder of their navy blue uniforms bore a patch—a Mexican flag on one shoulder and a "Policia" insignia on the other.

Officer Ruiz straightened the bill of his cap and stood by an open car door. His fingers flicked at a gun holster on his right hip as he surveyed the village. At length the two officers proceeded to the closed front door of Cesar's house.

A gray sedan containing two men in suits drove up and parked behind the police car. The two officers glanced back at the sedan.

Diaz spoke in a near-whisper. "What's he doing here?"

"He's way off the reservation on this one," Ruiz said.

A tall, gaunt, middle-aged man with a square jaw and stone face emerged from the sedan. The man wore a white fedora and amber aviator sunglasses. A thin moustache framed his upper lip and a white silk handkerchief peeked out of his jacket pocket. The driver, wearing in an open-collar shirt under a suit jacket, remained in the car.

Ruiz addressed the man in the white fedora. "Detective Barojas, we were about to interview the boy."

Barojas scanned the village and joined the two officers at the door. He spoke in a gravelly baritone. "After you."

Diaz knocked and Rosa opened the door. Her eyes were bloodshot and her eyelids shiny and swollen. She wiped her nose with a handkerchief.

"You are the victim's daughter?" Ruiz asked.

"Yes."

"I'm Officer Ruiz. This is Officer Diaz and he is Detective Barojas. We are sorry for the events of last night. We will do everything we can to find the monster who did this to your family."

Rosa sniffled and brushed away a tear. "Thank you."

"Is your son home? We'd like to ask him a couple questions."

"This is not the best time."

Ruiz withdrew an envelope from his shirt pocket and held up a mug shot of Ramos. "Do you know this man?"

"Yes. I mean, I don't know him, but we have met."

"What is your relationship?"

"He was a guest at the hotel where I work. He was cordial—a gentleman, at first. Gave me big tips—biggest tips I ever got. We met for a drink. That's it."

"So no further contact?"

"Well, yes, he came here recently. I don't know how he found us. Nobody finds this place. I assume he followed me."

"You did not invite him?" Barojas asked.

"No."

"What did he want?" Ruiz asked.

"Take a guess. He was drunk. He struck me and papa threw him out. That was the last time we saw him."

"Until last night," Diaz said.

"Ramos is a mystery man," Ruiz said. "He's been arrested many times, but he never served a day in jail. Moves around a lot, goes by different names. We suspect he's involved with a criminal organization."

"We don't know why he came to the coast," Diaz said. "Maybe he's lying low."

Cesar appeared at his mother's side. His eyes were red and his hair disheveled.

"They want to ask you some questions," Rosa said. "It's up to you."

Cesar nodded.

Ruiz showed Cesar the photo of Ramos. "That him?"

Cesar nodded and looked down.

Diaz knelt on one knee. "Remember anything new? Any details that you may have forgotten to mention last night?"

"No."

"I wish to speak with the boy," Barojas said. "Privately." The two officers turned and sauntered to their car.

Barojas stepped inside the dusky house. He did not

remove his sunglasses.

Cesar, Rosa and Barojas sat at the dining table. Barojas leaned on his elbows and kneaded his wide flat chin with his knuckles, then stood and paced. "This place takes me back. I grew up in a home very much like yours."

Barojas peered into a steaming pot on the hotplate. "What's this? Don't tell me. Pinto beans and corn, with tomato, jalapeño, pepper, and onions."

"Not onions—chives," Rosa said.

Barojas leaned over the simmering pot and inhaled deeply. "Very subtle, señora. Where do you find chives?"

"The hotel. Leftovers from the kitchen. They would be thrown away if I did not take them."

A faint smile creased the detective's lips. "That is not a crime, señora."

Barojas cracked his knuckles and resumed pacing. "My mama cooked all of our meals on a hotplate. We had very little, but that never stopped her from making the most delicious meals. I can taste them even now."

Barojas stopped pacing and looked at Cesar. "This man, Ramos—you are positive it was Ramos who took your grandfather's life?"

"Yes."

"You would know him if you saw him again?"

Cesar nodded.

"There is no doubt in your mind?"

"No."

Barojas sat and leaned close to the boy.

"Would you testify to that in a court of law, even if it meant putting your family in danger?"

"Yes."

"He is a dangerous man. You are not a little afraid?"

Cesar shook his head and studied his amber reflection in the detective's sunglasses. He longed for distance from the pain in his heart, like his disembodied reflection.

"You do not have to worry about Cesar," Rosa said. "He always does what is right."

Barojas slammed his hand on the table. Cesar and Rosa jumped and the bouquet of pink plastic roses bounced on its side.

Outside, the two officers glanced at the door. "What was that?" Diaz asked.

Ruiz spoke in a low voice. "Barojas is an old school head-knocker. His methods aren't subtle. I almost feel sorry for them."

"Maybe I should go in."

The older officer scowled and spat. "You like your job?"

Diaz shrugged.

"Well, I like mine, so you just stay put."

"You're almost retired, Ruiz. I'm just getting started. I have ambitions."

"I'm not retired yet. You just keep your damn ambitions to your damn self."

Diaz sagged against the car and folded his arms.

Inside the house, Detective Barojas said to Cesar, "You and me, we are from the same tribe. Nothing is given to us. We must fight for everything. I can see it in your eyes. You are a fighter, like me."

Barojas leaned back and drummed his fingers on the

table. "If Ramos is connected to a criminal enterprise, he is a threat to his organization. It may not tolerate behavior that draws attention." Barojas stood and resumed pacing. Cesar's and Rosa's eyes followed the detective as he orbited the table.

"I'm not saying you can't trust the federal police—there are honest men among them who cannot be bought for any price—but the cartels have great influence. If you see Ramos again I want you to speak with me directly."

"Cesar, listen to the detective," Rosa said. "You cannot trust anyone."

Barojas fished a business card out of his shirt pocket. He flipped it on the table and produced a gold pen. He leaned over the card and scratched a phone number on the back, and slid the card between the salt and pepper shakers.

Barojas reached into a jacket pocket and withdrew a thick wad of bills. He peeled a dozen bills off the roll and stacked them on the table one-by-one. "For the funeral."

Rosa stared at the money. "So much. I don't know what to say."

"Say nothing, señora. My condolences to you and your family."

Barojas looked at Cesar.

"You are under my personal protection."

Barojas opened the door and stepped into the noonday sun.

8

The funeral service for Abuelito was held at the Rio Seco mission near the plaza. Abuelito's closed coffin rested on two sawhorses in the center aisle. Cesar was seated by the aisle and his hand lay on the simple wooden casket. Rosa and Maria sat in the front pew. In the back of the small church, three rows behind Cesar, Miguel, Guillermo and another fisherman wore clean buttoned-up shirts. Outside, several federal police officers stood watch.

A middle-aged priest wearing white vestments stood in front of the altar, draped with a purple runner, and said the mass. Behind the altar a cracked wooden crucifix hung in an alcove.

The priest spoke of Abuelito's dedication to his family and his work, and said his exemplary life had shown others how to be true servants of God. "It is not always clear to us why things happen the way they do, but God's plan for our lives is perfect. No one can change His will."

When it was her turn to speak, Rosa fought back tears. "Papa would still be with us if he was not brave and did not love his family. He had the biggest heart of any man I ever knew. He was generous and kind, even to the smallest fish in the ocean."

Rosa returned to her seat and the priest asked Cesar, "Would you like to say anything?" Cesar shook his head.

After the service, Maria drove Cesar and Rosa to the cemetery—a neglected plot with small, simple headstones on an otherwise barren, sunbaked hillside. The priest commended Abuelito to God's mercy and prayed over his coffin as it was lowered into the ground. Rosa's eyes swam with tears as workers shoveled dirt into the grave.

The priest asked Rosa, "Can I do anything else, señora?" She shook her head and did not look up. The priest walked to the truck that delivered Abuelito's coffin and climbed in, and the truck rumbled away.

Maria sat in her station wagon and rolled down the front windows. After a while she lay across the front seat and fell asleep.

Cesar sat on the hillside in a weary daze and stared at the valley below. A ragged line of brush and browning palms traced a dry creek that ran like a river two seasons earlier. A pair of hawks circled each other high above the ravine, gliding on thermal winds.

Cesar did not notice the hawks or the dry palms or even the bulging hill opposite the cemetery. The boy's soul was steeped in melancholy and his mind wandered to memories of his days on the ocean with Abuelito and the shared routines that gave his life purpose and joy. His world was forever changed and Cesar knew he would have to find his own way, as had his grandfather.

Maria's snores summoned the boy and his mother to the station wagon. Rosa gently awakened her friend and they drove away.

When Cesar and Rosa returned home a knot of dried flowers bound with a faded blue ribbon hung on their door. Rosa looked across the street. Señora Muñoz and Fatima smiled faintly and nodded.

9

Officers Ruiz and Diaz visited Rosa and Cesar every few days and briefed them on their investigation. Their updates were always the same—Ramos had not been seen since the fateful night in Rio Seco and there were no new leads. The officers reminded Cesar that as an eyewitness to his grandfather's murder he could put Ramos away for a long time. Cesar prayed for the opportunity.

After several weeks the officers' visits tapered off. During their final visit, Officer Ruiz speculated that Ramos had left the area and would not likely be seen again. "He doesn't dare come back here. If he does, it will be the end for him."

Cesar and Rosa watched the police car roll up the road and disappear over the rise.

10

Rosa could not escape an unshakable conviction that she bore as much responsibility for Abuelito's death as Ramos. Convinced of her guilt, Rosa readily surrendered herself to whatever torments God might deem suitable punishment for her wrongdoing. She did not sleep at night, and though the pillows that she changed at the hotel felt like they weighed a hundred pounds, she missed not a single day of work. She welcomed her penance and committed deeply to suffering the fullness of God's unerring judgment.

Rosa reviewed her life without fear and her mistakes besieged her like an apocalyptic flood. Torrents of forgotten selfish acts reintroduced themselves and she lived them anew, each one bringing unremitting waves of shame. She prayed not for forgiveness, but for a thoroughly abrasive cleansing of her sins by any necessary means—up to and including her own death. She did not even feel worthy of such prayers.

Rosa conferred with the mission priest in Rio Seco and resolved to atone for her sins. She renounced drinking and dancing and all other terrestrial temptations that might obscure her righteous path, and gave herself completely over to God.

Deeper still was her resolve that Cesar would not suffer the same precarious life of a poor, illiterate fisherman in a no-name village as had her father. No, Cesar would accomplish great things such as no member of her family had ever achieved.

While Rosa grappled with her regrets and plotted a better life for her son, Cesar struggled to reconcile his own lapses in judgment. Why did I not heed Abuelito? he asked himself again and again. Abuelito is never wrong.

The boy's thoughts drifted back to the ghastly night in the plaza and he reimagined the tragic events with a terrible clarity. In his mind, he saw Abuelito cross the plaza and zigzag between dancers and mariachis, and move through ranks of onlookers.

He watched his grandfather pass a teenage boy and his sweetheart, a dreamy girl in a white cotton blouse embroidered with a tangle of flowers. The boy's arms folded around her waist and her head leaned against his chest as they swayed in time with the music.

Cesar saw Abuelito smile and bow his head as he passed three stout women who danced in place, their faded cotton dresses holding close to their soft round shoulders. The boy followed his grandfather around a family represented by four generations, from infants swaddled in rebozos to its proud 80-year-old matriarca.

Cesar watched Abuelito pause at a taco cart where a woman stooped over several pots, her head engulfed in steam. She spooned beans and chicken and beef into soft corn tortillas, and topped them with cilantro, onions, white cheese, and green and red sauces. Abuelito ordered three tacos and paid the woman, and bowed his head.

Cesar watched Abuelito turn and move through the crowd. Above, the fountain's fineal glowed in the sun's last golden light. The boy called out to his grandfather, but he was already gone.

While his mother worked at the hotel, Cesar spent his days alone at home. The boy rarely left his house, not because he felt unsafe—he now understood that one's safety could never be assured—but because the house was his closest connection to Abuelito.

Cesar ached to drive the coast road with his grandfather once more and motor out of the harbor before sunrise and catch caballitos. The boy cleaned the fishing gear in Abuelito's annex and arranged it so that it would be ready to pack at a moment's notice. He felt better for a while, but his spirits soon dipped to their lowest ebb. The pictures of blue marlin on his bedroom walls reminded him of his once optimistic, but now uncertain future. He ripped the pictures down and stuffed them in a bag.

One afternoon Cesar looked through the brochures on Abuelito's bedside table that were given to them by the university students. He examined an image of a dead seabird, its exposed gullet filled with a rainbow of undigested bits of plastic that starved the bird to death. He studied a photo of a grotesquely deformed sea turtle, corseted by a plastic band that ensnared the turtle when it was young and around which its bulging front and back halves had grown to maturity. The pictures must have saddened Abuelito, Cesar thought. Maybe Abuelito kept them at his bedside to remind him of his duty to the providing sea. The boy wished he could do something about the plastic in the ocean. In time I will make a difference, he thought.

Cesar pulled the sport fishing magazines out of the crate and a thick envelope fell from one onto the floor. The boy opened the envelope and discovered that it was stuffed with cash. This money was intended for my birthday, he thought. Abuelito planned to charter a white boat with this money so I could catch a blue marlin.

Cesar stared at the cash and thought about the fishing trip that would never be. He tucked the envelope inside the magazine and placed it back in the crate.

One morning Cesar sat on the bluff and watched the languid surge of water in and out of the cove. Plastic debris littered the narrow beach and high tides had deposited more trash in crevices between the rocks. Maybe a storm will wash it all away, he thought, but if I don't do something about it myself the plastic may never leave the cove.

Cesar scurried down the narrow path to the beach and kicked off his sandals. He began picking up plastic trash and piling it at a high point in the rocks, well beyond the water's immediate reach. His pace quickened and the pile grew. He even chased plastic debris into the surf before it escaped back into the sea.

By mid-afternoon Cesar had assembled a tall pile of

plastic trash. He and Abuelito had always carted their garbage to the drums at the harbor and now it dawned on the boy that he no longer had any means of removing the trash. I must find a way, he thought. It is my duty.

Cesar tugged his T-shirt off and dove into the warm surf. The water soothed his sun-broiled skin and tired muscles. He took a deep breath and dipped under the surface, and swayed with the gentle ocean surge.

He surfaced and glanced up at the bluff, and his heart jumped. For a moment Cesar thought he saw Ramiro Ramos staring down at him. He wiped hair and water from his eyes and when he looked again he saw only the vacant edge of the bluff and stark blue sky beyond.

During the next week Cesar scoured years of accumulated grime out of the interior of Abuelito's VW bus, and then scrubbed the bus's engine and exterior until they sparkled. Sometimes he sat behind the steering wheel and imagined driving the bus north to the harbor. His feet barely reached the floor, and he didn't know how to use the stick shift anyway, so he was content to just imagine the journey. In just a matter of time he would drive the bus to the harbor. And for the first time in many days the boy was buoyed with hope.

Cesar was showering behind his house when he heard the familiar toot of Maria's station wagon. He toweled off and tugged on his jeans, then ran to the front of the house and watched the station wagon go over the rise.

He entered the house as his mother set a box of groceries on the counter. She turned to her son and smiled. "I have a surprise for you. Close your eyes and open your hand."

Cesar shut his eyes and extended his hand. He felt small smooth object placed in his palm.

"Okay, you can look."

Cesar opened his eyes and beheld a black flip phone. He unfolded the phone and a blank screen lit up.

"An early birthday present from Maria. Remember to say thank you."

Rosa fished a phone charger out of a pocket and handed it to Cesar. "Almost forgot."

"I don't think these work here," he said.

"Someday you will need it. Besides, it's progress. That is how you should think about your life—making progress."

An hour later Rosa served burritos and they sat for dinner. "I sold the bus," Rosa said with casual indifference. She did not look up from her plate.

Cesar stopped eating mid-bite. "What?"

Rosa continued eating and did not look up. "I sold the bus. To a co-worker. Her husband needs it to carry supplies." Cesar stared unblinking at his mother until she picked up her plate and fled his gaze.

"It's done," she said, rinsing her plate in the sink.

"You can't sell Abuelito's bus. It is his bus, not yours."

Rosa wheeled around and glared at her son.

"I need the money to buy a regular car. How else am I going to take you to the bus stop each morning?"

"I am not going to school."

"I will need to pay for books. Maybe a computer."

"I told you—I am not going to school."

"You are going to school. I already enrolled you. Classes start in three weeks."

"Abuelito would never make me go to school."

"Your future was not his decision. It's not too late for you to make something of yourself. You should want a better life."

"My life is here, by the ocean—just like Abuelito." Cesar stormed into his bedroom and slammed the door. His half-eaten burrito lay on the plate.

The next morning, Cesar watched the VW bus rumble away for the last time.

During the next several days Cesar's disappointment dissipated when he realized that he could buy his own VW bus in time. After all, the boy already had Abuelito's savings for the white boat, money that was specifically intended for his benefit.

Cesar begged his mother to take him with her and her co-workers to the harbor on their way to work. The harbor was along the way, he reasoned. He could spend the day tending to the skiff. Rosa was leery of Cesar's fondness for the harbor, but she relented to his pleas— what difference would a final visit make?—and one morning Cesar scrambled over the backseat of Maria's station wagon into the rear compartment.

Maria drove north and glanced in the rearview mirror. "I hear you are going to attend school, Cesar. Going to learn how to read and write and add numbers."

Juanita, seated next to Rosa in the backseat, said, "So you can count up all the money you're going to make."

Cesar gazed west out the window, catching glimpses of moonlight shimmering on the ocean between hills and dunes.

"School starts in two weeks," Rosa said. "The teacher says Cesar will need a year or two to catch up with students in his age group, but if he works hard he will be fine."

"Think you can do that, Cesar?" Maria asked.

Cesar did not hear Maria's question. In his mind he was driving up the coast in the VW bus with Abuelito.

A familiar tingle of anticipation welled up in the boy as the station wagon approached the harbor. Soon he would see the skiff again and hear the sweet hum of the Evinrude—music to his ears. Maybe he would take the skiff for a jaunt around the harbor.

Maria pulled onto the shoulder of the coast road across from the harbor entrance and dropped the boy off. Rosa reminded Cesar that they would return for him before sunset. "Be on time or you will spend the night here." Rosa would never leave her son overnight at the harbor, of course. She was only demonstrating her parenting skills for her friends.

The sun had not yet risen when Cesar walked into the harbor's shadowy parking lot. As he tramped down the last dock, he sensed that something was amiss even before he reached the skiff. When he arrived he saw that the Evinrude was missing. He stepped into the skiff and sank to the middle seat, and stared at the vacant transom.

Missing, too, was the red gasoline can that fueled the motor. Only the splintery wooden oars and a length of yellow plastic rope remained.

Unburdened of the Evinrude the skiff sat high in the water and bucked its tie lines, eager, like Cesar, to venture onto the ocean again. The boy watched a fisherman motor out of the harbor in a small boat and listened to the motor putter away until sounds of the skiff slapping the water reclaimed the berth.

At dawn Cesar climbed the sand dunes on the harbor's west side and looked north and south. The shore curved away in both directions and disappeared in marine mist.

The boy felt the sunrise on his back. He lay on the warming sand, closed his eyes, and fell asleep.

The thundering chop of a low-flying helicopter jolted Cesar awake as it passed beneath the late-morning sun. The boy shielded his eyes from the stinging spray of sand and watched the helicopter shrink down the coast until it faded from sight.

Cesar strolled along the beach, kicking up plastic litter when he didn't watch his step. From the top of the dunes the coast appeared pristine—only clean white sand dunes for miles on end. Up close, garbage was dense and unending.

Cesar looked around to assess whether the trash that he and Abuelito carried away had reduced its volume, and discovered that he was standing on the very spot where they had only recently filled their buckets. Now there was more debris than before.

Cesar spotted the corner of a half-buried plastic produce sack jutting from the sand and waving in the breeze as if beckoning the boy. He uncovered the sack and began filling it with plastic debris. When it was full, he slung the sack over his shoulder and carried it over the dunes and around the harbor, and poured its contents on the ground next to the overflowing steel drums. He returned to the beach and refilled the sack, and poured the debris on the rising pile by the drums. For several hours Cesar traipsed back and forth between the beach and the mounting pile of plastic trash, filling and emptying the sack many times.

In the late afternoon the white boats returned. Cesar reburied the sack on top of a dune for future use and raced across the ridge and around the harbor. He watched giddy tourists debark from the white boats and display their catches for photos before crew gutted and filleted the fish.

Cesar recognized a ruddy captain who often bought baitfish from Abuelito. A white mustache hovered like a billowed cloud over his mouth. Cesar marched down the dock and stood beside the white boat until the captain noticed the boy. "Hey, there. Where's your grampa?"

"He is not here."

"No? Where's he at?"

"He died."

"Sorry to hear that. Good man, your grampa. I've been buying bait from him since before you were born. Guess I'll have to get it someplace else."

Cesar buried his hands in his pockets and waited. "Need something?" the captain asked with an air of suspicion.

"Will you take me fishing for blue marlin?"

The captain's brow furrowed and his face tightened. "I don't know, son. For one thing, it's expensive."

"I have money." Cesar had carried Abuelito's savings to the harbor like a propitious talisman. He gave the wad in his pocket a squeeze for reassurance.

The captain placed his hands on his hips and smiled. "Let's talk about it when you're a little bigger."

"I am almost ten."

"You just keep growing. Right now I got work that needs to get done." The captain directed a crewmember to wash down the rear deck. Cesar turned and slumped away.

"Hey, what was your grampa's name, son?" The question surprised Cesar. He watched his grandfather sell his baitfish to the captain countless times. Why hadn't the captain asked before? A pointed comment rose to the boy's lips, but he swallowed it and continued down the dock. "Sorry about your grampa, son. Good man, your grampa."

Cesar approached several more captains and asked them if he could buy a day of blue marlin fishing on their white boats, but he heard the same objections—too small, too young, too expensive, too anything the skeptical captains could think of to disengage from the boy. "Come back with your daddy and we'll talk about it," one said. Another offered Cesar coins, which he refused. The captains were not accustomed to chartering their boats to little boys with patched jeans and crooked haircuts.

Cesar saw the El Bucanero returning to port. He waved and Miguel tooted his horn. Cesar raced down the parking lot and met the boat as it pulled up to the dock. He held the El Bucanero's bow steady as Miguel nosed it into the lineup and cut the inboard engine, which belched twice before it came to rest. Guillermo joined his father on the rear deck and wiped his hands with a filthy rag that contributed even more grime to his dirty hands.

"Good to see you, my friend," Miguel said. "How did you get here? Did you fly?"

"Mama dropped me off. She will pick me up later."

"What have you been doing all day?"

"Cleaning the beach. There is a lot of trash."

Guillermo grinned. "I figured that's what you'd done."

Cesar asked Miguel, "Did you have a good day?"

"Wonderful day. See for yourself."

Miguel opened the metal cooler. Cesar leaped aboard the El Bucanero and peered inside. Albacore rose to the top.

Cesar smiled and nodded. "They're beautiful."

"They will make many delicious meals. Want to buy one? I will give you a good price."

Cesar shoved his hands in his pockets and stared at the albacore.

Miguel patted Cesar on the back. "Maybe I will bring a fish to your house. Say, is your mama seeing anyone special?"

"You are just going to give him a fish?" Guillermo asked.

Miguel pinched Cesar's shoulder and closed the cooler. "Maybe next time."

Miguel and Guillermo toted gear down the dock. "Back in a minute," Miguel said.

"Don't steal none of the tuna," Guillermo said.

Cesar glanced around the boat. The leather captain's chair was ripping at the seams, the wooden steering wheel was rubbed raw, and electrical tape held instruments in place. The boy felt a twinge of sympathy for the vessel and hoped it might yet see better days.

The cabin door was ajar and Cesar looked inside. On the floor, a propeller blade peeked out from under a plastic tarp. Cesar entered the cabin and lifted the tarp, and beheld the Evinrude and red gas can.

Cesar heard Guillermo shout. "Hey—what are you doing?" Cesar stepped out of the cabin and saw Miguel and Guillermo hurrying up the dock.

"I paid your mama a fair price," Miguel said before he reached the boat.

Cesar's mind raced. Why didn't mama ask my permission to sell the motor? It was Abuelito's motor. It should be mine now.

Cesar closed the cabin door and met Miguel and Guillermo on the rear deck. "She should not have sold it to you. It isn't for sale."

"That's between you and your mama," Miguel said. "I made a fair offer and she accepted it. A deal's a deal. If it makes you happy I will give you an albacore. No charge."

"If I return your money will you return the Evinrude?"

"I have plans for this motor."

"What plans?"

Miguel opened the cooler lid and brought out an albacore. "You like this one?"

"What plans?"

"I can sell it for a good profit."

"It is not for sale. I will speak to mama." Cesar stepped off the boat and strode down the dock.

"Our business is done, Cesar. A deal's a deal."

"Don't you dare come back," Guillermo said. He glared at his father. "I warned you about him. He's a garbage-eating mongrel."

Miguel slid the albacore into the cooler and smiled. "Relax, Gui. Don't worry about Cesar."

The sun was touching the horizon when Maria's station wagon pulled up to the edge of the coast road where Cesar waited. Hours earlier Miguel's truck sped out of the harbor parking lot and sprayed dust and gravel on the boy, and Guillermo made a pointed gesture out the window.

Cesar had plenty of time to think about his new circumstances. He thought about the Evinrude and the VW bus, and wondered if Rosa planned to sell the skiff—or if she had already sold it. And Abuelito's fishing gear? Not hers to sell! What value would it have, anyway? Little to anyone, except Cesar. Abuelito's fishing gear was the boy's most valued connection to his grandfather. He handled it nearly as often as Abuelito had—almost daily. Certainly it was as much his as it was his grandfather's. Mama would not dare sell Abuelito's fishing gear, he thought. Or would she?

Maria's station wagon pulled up and Cesar crawled in the back.

"Hope you didn't work too hard," Maria said.

"Did you miss us?" Rosa asked.

Cesar remained silent as he watched the harbor disappear from view through the rear window.

"Cat got your tongue?" Maria asked.

The school bus roared by the station wagon. Cesar saw students laughing and cavorting in the bus's back window.

"You missed your bus," Maria said, but the only bus Cesar was thinking about was his grandfather's.

When they arrived home Cesar went directly into Abuelito's shed to confirm that the fishing gear remained where he left it. The deep sea fishing rod hung over the bed, the students' brochures lay on the bedside table, and buckets sat in a tidy stack in the corner. Nothing had changed.

Cesar entered the house. Rosa sat at the table and tugged her shoes off. "Something on your mind?"

"Take a wild guess."

Rosa sighed and took a deep breath. "I had to sell the motor. You need things for school. Many things—things I cannot afford. Clothes, books—they are more important than that rusty old motor. You need to be in a classroom, not on a fishing boat. Be grateful you can get an education so you will not have to fish for the rest of your life, or change dirty, disgusting beds in hotels all day. You are lucky. You can have a better life."

Cesar sat at the table. "I am not going to school. I

am a fisherman, just like Abuelito."

"You have no right to complain. You will go to school. Someday you will thank me for thinking about your future."

Cesar went into his room and started to close his door, and held up. His eyes smoldered. "How much did he pay?"

Rosa folded her arms across her chest. "I only want the best for you. See it for what it is."

"How much?"

"Full asking price."

"Miguel is a shark. He cheated you."

"What do you know?"

Cesar closed his door and lay on his bed. Later, he ignored his mother's dinner call. He thought about Abuelito, who surely would have protected him from attending school. His mother allowed Ramos into their home and into their lives. It was she who caused all of his troubles. Now she was only adding to his miseries.

Cesar reflected on his grandfather's life on the ocean, learning the ways of the fish—of caballitos and flying fish and swordfish and marlin. If I go to school I will never catch a blue marlin, he thought. In his mind he saw his grandfather, younger and stronger, standing on the rear deck of a white boat fighting a trophy blue marlin with his deep sea rod, the captain and crew cheering him on. Abuelito would give line when the marlin made runs and reel in the slack when the fish jumped and shook its head to slough the hook. Abuelito knew the ways of the blue marlin and now Cesar would have to learn them by himself.

Cesar thought about the profound sorrow that Abuelito must have felt when he was left behind by his parents, how he set out to find his father and bring him home, and was robbed and beaten. He thought about how his grandfather climbed the hill and hid while his damaged body recovered, and how he was almost eaten by coyotes. And he thought about Abuelito's vision, how the sea spoke to him and told him not to worry, that the sea would provide.

In that moment, Cesar knew that the sea would take care of him, too.

11

J ust before midnight Cesar slid his feet into his sandals in near-total darkness. He cracked his door and peered into the front room. His mother's bedroom door was closed and the overhead light was off. Only a small lamp by the sink glowed, left on by Rosa to discourage potential intruders. Cesar tiptoed to the dining table and saw a burrito on a plate by his chair. He picked up the burrito and unlatched the front door, and stepped outside into the warm night air, closing the door softly behind him.

Cesar entered Abuelito's annex, almost completely black except for a pale wash of moonlight that fell on the plywood floor through the open hatch. He took a bite of the cold burrito and set it on a shelf in the bookcase.

Cesar lifted an empty bucket off the stack, which tipped and banged hard on the floor. The boy stood still and listened. Hearing nothing, he set the bucket down and placed his burrito inside, and righted the fallen stack. He added the spooled caballito rigging and a fillet knife to the empty bucket, and leaned a light fishing rod by the hatch. Finally, he stepped up on Abuelito's bed and lifted his grandfather's deep sea rod off the nails. Cesar tied the two rods together with a small length of rope, grabbed the bucket, and slipped out the hatch.

The boy walked up the gray dirt road and at the top of the rise he looked back toward his house. For the first time since Abuelito passed he experienced the same exhilarating feeling of anticipation that he always felt when he traveled with his grandfather to the harbor. Then he continued over the rise to claim his destiny.

Cesar polished off the burrito before he reached the coast road. He figured he would arrive at the harbor well before daybreak, important because of his pending business with Miguel and the El Bucanero. He felt sudden apprehension when he thought about arriving any later and quickened his pace. His plan would fail if Miguel reached the harbor first.

At this early hour the hills and sand dunes lining the still-warm coast road were charcoal gray. Cesar passed below a hillside resort and heard revelers partying outside one of the rooms. A bottle shattered a few feet behind the boy and broken glass glanced off his legs. He knew that he was not a target, not in this darkness.

High beam headlights of southbound vehicles temporarily blinded the boy, but they were few at this hour. A semi-truck passed close. Cesar slapped his hand on his head to secure his cap and discovered that he had left it behind. No matter. He would tie one of the rags that Abuelito kept in the skiff around his head to protect it from the harsh sun.

Cesar thought about Abuelito's trek along the same

route to find his father many years earlier. Now he was walking in his grandfather's footsteps. The boy felt no fear because he knew that the sea would provide, but he was also sad that Abuelito paid so steep a price to learn the same lesson.

These thoughts kept Cesar company as he pushed on through the balmy night. And then he set his mind to the work ahead.

12

The harbor was still and the restaurants dark when Cesar tramped into the empty parking lot. The boy estimated that he had at least one full hour to attend to his tasks.

The plastic trash that he carted from the beach the previous day sat in a shadowy clump next to the drums. Seagulls that had settled on the warm dunes for the night were silent, save for an occasional territorial squabble.

Cesar walked down the last dock and set his fishing gear down by the skiff. He surveyed the harbor and listened—sometimes fishermen bedded down on their boats—and then proceeded to the El Bucanero, tied up at the end of the dock. The boy glanced around and took a furtive step onto the rear deck.

He turned the doorknob on the cabin door, but it was locked. He gave the knob a hard tug and the door held fast. Just my luck, he thought. The only thing on the boat that is in good working order.

Cesar peered in the door's window but the cabin was dark. He traced a vertical crack in the window with his finger and slipped a sandal off. He laid the sole over the crack and punched the sandal, but the window did not break. The boy punched again, harder. The window still did not yield and he shook his hand in pain.

Cesar faced away from the door and repositioned the sandal. He drew his arm straight out and swung his elbow back. The cabin window exploded and glass sprinkled on the floor inside.

Cesar reached through the broken window, turned the doorknob, and opened the door. He peered around the harbor once more and stepped inside the cabin, and waited a moment for his eyes to adjust to the darkness.

The boy flung the tarp aside and moved the half-full red gas can to the door. Another gas can, this one larger, sat on the floor toward the bow. He picked up the can and its weight told him that it was nearly full. The extra gas will carry the skiff a great distance, he thought. I can replenish it later.

Cesar toted the two sloshing cans to the skiff. He set the larger can on the floor next to the transom and placed his grandfather's half-empty red can in the bow.

The boy returned to the El Bucanero and reentered the cabin. The Evinrude had always outweighed Cesar by a considerable amount and he had never moved it by himself. Abuelito always carried the heavier end—the main engine—and the boy carried the propeller end. Cesar had grown over an inch during the last year and he hoped that he would be able to move the Evinrude by himself. The boy squatted and hugged the Evinrude's power head. He raised the motor off the floor with a grunt and balanced it upright on the skeg.

A car rolled into the parking lot and Cesar froze.

Tires ground the gravel surface as it slowed to a stop near the last dock. The engine idled for a moment and stopped.

Silence hung heavy in the air until the muffled laughter of a man and a woman broke the quietude. The car started and rolled away, and the boy took a deep breath.

Cesar jockeyed the motor to the cabin door, broken glass crunching underfoot, and maneuvered it up one step onto the rear deck. He propped the Evinrude against the rail and closed the door.

Cesar stepped onto the dock and wrapped his arms around the Evinrude, and heaved it over the rail. He walked the motor backwards, half-dragging it down the dock. His arms ached, but he knew he must bring the Evinrude to the skiff now or miss his opportunity.

The boy redoubled his efforts, lugging the motor with every ounce of his strength. When Cesar reached the skiff, he lowered the Evinrude to the edge of the dock, hopped in the boat, and wrestled the motor onto the transom. He secured the bracket mount and tilted the prop down into the water.

The boy brought the fishing gear aboard, then connected the gas line to the large gas can and primed the pump. He yanked the Evinrude's pull cord and the motor hummed to life. Seagulls took wing and shrieked their confusion at the early-hour disturbance. Cesar cast off and guided the skiff toward the harbor mouth.

The rush of pure sea air and uninterrupted ocean expanse invigorated the weary boy. The caballitos were running and soon his bucket would be filled with baitfish that would tempt a blue marlin.

Cesar had never taken the skiff a significant distance by himself. Abuelito promised the boy that he would captain the skiff when he was ready. Cesar believed that Abuelito would agree his moment had arrived. He smiled, confident that his grandfather was riding with him as he motored north. This way, Abuelito said. The caballitos are waiting for you.

A quarter-moon glowed silver-white against azure sky and a fringe of yellow light on the eastern hills foretold the sunrise. The boy was ahead of schedule. He studied familiar landmarks to his starboard—the wide saddle between two sharp peaks in the hills, the resort with its signature blue lights, the village on the point, identifiable by two bare light bulbs, one dim and one bright. He factored the absence of wind and a modest southern current, veered west, and resumed a northern heading parallel to the coast.

Headlights on the coast road were beginning to form horizontal stacks behind slower-moving vehicles. Cesar wondered if the school bus might be among them. Don't worry about the school bus, Abuelito said. You don't have to go to school if you don't want to. You're a fisherman. You can fish every day for the rest of your life.

Cesar consulted his landmarks and slowed the skiff. The water was calm and he could almost feel the caballitos rising to greet him. He shut off the motor and the skiff drifted, and he heard the distant break of small waves on the shore. The boy untied the rope that bound his rods and pulled the spooled caballito rig out of the bucket. He unrolled the feathered jigs and hitched the rig to the light fishing rod, and filled the bucket with water.

He was ready to inherit his grandfather's work.

Cesar pressed his thumb on the spool of the open-face reel and swung his line behind his back. He flung it forward and released his thumb. Line whirred off the reel and the feathered jigs plunked in the water thirty yards away. Cesar fed line from his reel with his free hand and let the rig descend longer than usual in case the fish might be deep. He pressed his thumb on the spool when the rig reached depth and felt the line tighten. As he reeled the rig in, he slowly raised and dipped his rod to make the feathered jigs swim, inviting the attention of hungry caballitos.

The rig arrived at the surface and Cesar cast again. He fed line from his reel as the rig sank. He resumed the up and down action with his rod and brought the rig back to the boat. The boy inspected the rig and found nothing amiss. He scanned the coast and confirmed the correct location. Am I too early? he wondered.

Make the jigs dance with smaller jerks, Abuelito said. It will make the caballitos ravenous.

Cesar cast again and waited. He pressed his thumb on the line when the rig reached depth and began reeling it in, this time bouncing his rod with short, quick movements.

A caballito struck hard and the rod bowed. Cesar held tight, surprised by the fish's strength. The taut line moved in a jittery circle where it met the water. Cesar took his time bringing the fish in, committing its methods to memory. When the caballito reached the surface the boy lifted it over the side of the skiff and lowered it into the bucket. He set his rod down and removed the hook from the fish's mouth, and covered the bucket with the wet rag. Cesar felt the approving nods of his grandfather. During the next ten minutes he brought in five more caballitos with only five casts.

Content with six frisky baitfish, Cesar laid his fishing rod down and yanked the starter rope, and the Evinrude purred. He aimed the skiff toward the horizon and motored west. Behind him the pink-and-orange glow behind the gray hills announced the dawn.

Less than an hour later Cesar was further from the coast than he and Abuelito had ever ventured. The skiff rose and fell as it met the long incoming swell, and Cesar felt the water cool and deepen beneath his feet. He looked back and saw the sun rising, as if it was watching the boy.

Abuelito once told Cesar about a shelf on the seafloor just beyond the horizon that dropped off into the deepest depths of the ocean. That's where the blue marlin sleep, Abuelito said, and where no fishing lines will reach. At daybreak the blue marlin would rise along the shelf wall in search of prey and today Cesar would be there to tempt them with fresh caballitos.

Cesar felt free—free of his mother's plans for his education, free of the boundaries defined by baitfish that kept his grandfather's skiff close to the coast, free of his past. Now Cesar would determine his own future, just as Abuelito had when he was a boy. He was certain that he would captain a white boat and fish for blue marlin one day, and teach his sons the ways of the sea.

The boy decided that he would move into Abuelito's

shed when he returned home. For the first time, he felt like his life was in perfect balance.

Cesar glanced back at the coast and was startled to discover that only the hazy hilltops were visible above the water. He gauged that they would disappear from view where the shelf fell away. There he would rig a caballito on Abuelito's deep sea fishing rod and offer it to a big blue marlin.

He had long dreamed of the day when he would catch his blue marlin and today was that day. Abuelito promised Cesar that he would accompany him on this journey, and the boy knew his grandfather was riding with him. Cesar felt at peace, but the sound of the Evinrude still comforted the boy.

Again Cesar looked back toward the hills and now he saw only the ocean horizon, where light blue sky met dark blue water. With no land in sight a strange new feeling took hold of the boy. He felt alone and vulnerable in this desolate, unfamiliar place.

Cesar cut the engine and reached for his grandfather's deep sea fishing rod. It felt heavier than before, imbued with new authority. Cesar removed the J-hook from the pitted rubber grip and swung it free. He cranked the handle of the corroded chrome reel and it balked and jammed after two turns. The boy jiggled the handle forward and backward until it rotated a full turn without jamming. He swung the dangling J-hook toward him and grabbed the metal leader.

Cesar raised the wet rag that covered his bucket and removed a wriggling caballito. He remembered when Abuelito showed him how to rig a live baitfish, using his hand and fingers to mimic a fish, needle and hook. Cesar lacked a needle to thread a line through the caballito's head and create a bridle on which to affix the hook, so he sewed the hook through the middle of the fish's upper mouth and forehead. It was not a secure rigging but Cesar figured that he would still have plenty of bait should the caballito slip off.

Cesar pressed his thumb on the spool of the open-face reel. He raised the rod and swung the baited caballito around his back. He drew the rod over his shoulder and cast the caballito forward, releasing his thumb. The reel seized and the line snapped with a crack. The caballito separated from the J-hook and sailed away from the skiff, glinting in the sun. The fish splashed in the water and flashed once before it swam out of sight.

Cesar stared at small concentric ripples left by the splash. At the end of his rod, the broken line whipped in a light offshore breeze. The boy seized the line and examined it. Tiny cracks scarred the oxidized plastic filament. He clutched a section of line with both hands and stretched it apart, and the line snapped easily.

Cesar struggled to crank the frozen reel, but it would not budge. He tossed the deep sea rod on the forward benches, hugged his shins, and lowered his head to his knees. Of course the line is bad, he thought. Abuelito has not used his deep sea rod for many years. I have missed my opportunity. I will wait a long time for another chance.

Now the sun was well above the eastern horizon. The skiff swiveled on the ocean surface as the offshore breeze picked up, nudging the boat westward. The temperature was also rising and Cesar tied a rag around his head. He leaned back against the side of the skiff as it rode the swells, rising gently over the crests and sliding into the long troughs. Exhausted by a sleepless night and fresh disappointment, Cesar closed his eyes. I'm still free, he thought. Today the ocean is mine and mine alone. Abuelito undertook a dangerous journey when he was young and he discovered his destiny. On this journey I, too, have realized my destiny. My path is not so different from Abuelito's. I will be a fisherman, just like him.

Cesar thought about his mother, toiling now in the hotel as she always had, six days out of seven. She would never understand the ocean, or Cesar's calling to fish for blue marlin. That was okay, as long as she did not try to take it away from him. In that case, the boy would just have to go his own way. For now he would enjoy his time alone on the sea, and when he returned home he would move into Abuelito's annex and the next stage of his life. His destiny was as clear as the cloudless sky.

Cesar stretched out on the bench and leaned his head against the edge of the boat, and fell fast asleep.

13

A mighty splash followed by a shower of seawater rocked the skiff and roused the boy from his sleep. Cesar sat up and looked around. A cloud of bubbles rose through roiled water next to the boat. Whitecaps had begun to form and the offshore wind had strengthened, but no breaking waves were in sight, not even small ones. The boy dismissed the odd phenomenon as a mere trick of nature. Just a big wave, he thought. He squinted up at the midday sun and estimated he had slept for two hours.

Cesar picked up the deep sea fishing rod and tried to turn the reel. He lost the J-hook earlier so he was not disappointed when the handle would not turn. He would take the reel apart when he returned home and clean and oil every piece, and restore it to its original condition. One afternoon Cesar watched Abuelito disassemble the VW bus engine and array the pieces across an old blanket, clean the parts that night, and reassemble the engine the next morning. And he remembered his astonishment when Abuelito turned the ignition key and the engine started right up. The reel would be easy to fix.

Cesar peeled the rag on the bucket back. The caballitos had lost their color and spirit. He slid his fingers down the side of the bucket. It was hot to the touch and he jerked his hand away.

"Thank you for joining me, my friends. You have done your part even if I have not done mine."

The boy raised the bucket and poured the caballitos into the ocean. They hovered in the water and their tails twitched. The fish gradually gathered together and moved under the skiff.

Cesar's attention shifted to his journey home. He decided to beach the skiff in the cove by his village, far away from the harbor where Miguel might try to reclaim the Evinrude and exact a price for the broken window. Cesar resolved to return the gas can, filled to the top, but Miguel would never again possess the Evinrude. The boy had stashed his longboard in a cleft in the bluff and there was still ample room to conceal the motor. The skiff could be left on the beach indefinitely. Few would find use for it.

A new feeling of confidence washed over the boy. Now I am a man, making decisions for myself, he thought. It is my life and I will live it as I wish. If mama chooses to go her own way, so be it. I can take care of myself. And the sea will always provide.

He tilted the Evinrude's propeller down and primed the motor.

"Cesar."

The boy heard Abuelito call his name from the bow. He turned and looked at the empty front bench. He resumed priming the motor and clutched the pull cord.

Again the boy heard Abuelito's voice: "Cast the light rod."

Cesar spun around and the bench was still empty. He imagined his grandfather sitting there, smiling and enjoying their shared adventure.

Cesar wondered what baitfish might be caught this far from shore. Flying fish? They are a favorite of the marlin, but I have not seen one all day. Sardines? Maybe so. Mackerel? Of course, mackerel! They roam far from the shore. Abuelito caught many blue marlin with mackerel.

If I am going to captain a white boat I will need to understand the mackerel, he thought. I will know the fish better when I catch one. Maybe mama and I will have mackerel for dinner. Two mackerel would be even better. And maybe one more for Señora Muñoz and Fatima.

Cesar loved the mackerel's strong oily flavor and his mouth watered at the thought. He had not eaten for many hours, but soon he would return to shore and, with any luck, bring fresh-caught mackerel home for dinner.

Cesar had only the caballito rig, still attached to his light fishing rod. He decided that it would be instructive to learn if mackerel would bite on the feathered jigs. Worth a few extra minutes to find out, he thought.

Cesar picked up the light fishing rod and pressed his thumb on the spool, and bounced the feathered jigs in the air to make sure they were not tangled. He raised the tip of the rod and brought the rig around his back, and cast with the wind. The rig splashed into the water a short distance away. Whitecaps quickly erased the ripples.

Cesar let the feathered jigs sink, as before when he fished for caballitos. He began reeling in the rig, twitching and dipping his rod until the jigs were visible ten feet below the surface of the clear blue water. Cesar drew the rig up and cast again, and continued the twitching action. After he reeled in the feathered jigs a third time he laid the rod across the benches and picked up the Evinrude's pull cord.

Cesar heard Abuelito's voice, as clearly as he could hear his own. "One more cast. Let the jigs sink."

"Abuelito, are you here?"

I am very hungry, Cesar thought. It is affecting my head.

The boy leaned back and made a final cast, and let the feathered jigs sink much deeper than before. He reeled them back to the skiff, twitching and dipping the rod.

A hard strike surprised Cesar and almost yanked the rod from his hands. Instead of reeling the fish directly to the boat, he played it, letting the fish take and give back line. After several runs, the fish's strength flagged and Cesar coaxed it toward the skiff.

The fish slashed sideways, but Cesar conceded no line and brought it close to the boat. When the boy saw the slender fish's triangular dorsal fin and vertical stripes on its silver-green back, he knew his catch was a mackerel.

The mackerel swam under the skiff and abruptly reversed course, bolting away from the boat with renewed vigor. It turned back once more and sped toward Cesar.

A long shadowy form rose from the depths. Cesar

leaned away as a spear pierced the surface and a billfish slammed into the mackerel.

The billfish rolled sideways, flashing incandescent colors that Cesar knew well. The billfish was a blue marlin. Longer and wider than the skiff, it was the biggest blue marlin that Cesar had ever seen, even in his sport fishing magazines.

With a flick of its tail the blue marlin shot away from the skiff, its dorsal fin cutting a tight wake on the surface. Line screamed off Cesar's reel and his light rod bent double. Fifty yards off the boy's starboard the fish leaped and shook its head with a fury. The chewed mackerel floated free, but a feathered jig remained embedded in its jaw.

The blue marlin crashed into the water and dove. Cesar's rod bowed and pointed the direction of the marlin's downward trajectory. Line flew off the spool and just when Cesar thought the fish would take his remaining line it turned and charged straight toward the skiff. Before Cesar could reel in the slackened line, the fish burst out of the water and arced over the boat.

Time slowed to a stop and sunlight filtered through the blue marlin like watery stained glass. Cesar examined the dark, sharp fins and tail that propelled the fish through the water with ease, and the long lethal bill that swatted and maimed its prey as it sliced through swarms of small fish. Icy-blue vertical stripes hung like icicles from the blue marlin's cobalt dorsal and tapered over its glittering gold flanks and silvery-white belly. In the blue marlin's gullet, the silhouettes of six caballitos lined up single-file.

The boy was entranced by the blue marlin's big sapphire pupil, ringed by a milky-blue iris. He peered into the fathomless eye and was transported to the deepest, darkest depths of the ocean, where mysterious creatures moved in the shadows. The deep was spookier and more dangerous than he had dared imagine, and he was thrilled.

Cesar wanted to stay and explore this strange new world, but he was snapped back to the skiff when the blue marlin completed its arc and crashed into the sea. The fish jumped once more and threw off the feathered jig, and then disappeared forever.

14

Cesar's eyes lingered on the turbulent water where the blue marlin reentered the sea. He watched the ripples dissipate until none remained. For a moment the boy was stricken with despair at losing the precious fish. He knew that he would never possess it again. Cesar reeled in the feathered jigs and laid the rod across the benches. Then he thrust his fists in the air and let out a long whoop. I did it, he thought. I caught the biggest blue marlin in the ocean!

Cesar started the motor and set a course for the coast. He was eager to tell his mother about his miracle fish, the biggest blue marlin ever. The blue marlin that he caught! Of course she would scold him for clinging to his dream of fishing, and the blue marlin might trouble her a little because she would know that Cesar's epic fish would only encourage his love of the sea. But that was okay. All that mattered to Cesar was that he and his grandfather knew that he caught the blue marlin. "Thank you, Abuelito," he said. "Thank you for guiding me to this blue marlin, our blue marlin. We did this together."

Now it was time to bring the skiff home, to its proper place in the cove, and conceal the Evinrude in the cleft in the bluff. Miguel could keep his gas can. Cesar would only need it today. He would not return to the deep water with the skiff again. No matter. In time he would captain a white boat and follow the billfish wherever they would lead him.

It occurred to the boy that Miguel might come to his house before he arrived home and confront his mother about the Evinrude, but she could not know that he took it. Rosa would defend him as only she could. She would return Miguel's money and cancel the sale, whether he liked it or not. That way Cesar could keep the Evinrude. Miguel might demand restitution for the broken window. But it was already broken, so why would any payment be necessary? If Miguel insists, I will sell the flip phone to pay for the window, the boy thought.

Cesar realized that he would happily pay any price for this magnificent day. He caught his blue marlin, and he was relieved that he did not have to fight the rare and beautiful fish until it nearly expired from fear and exhaustion. The blue marlin was now part of Cesar. It was his friend. Maybe more than a friend. It was family. Maybe more than family. He shuddered at the thought of his hook causing the blue marlin pain. Never again, he thought. Never again.

The sun was low in the west and the offshore wind was strong, spraying cool water off the whitecaps into Cesar's face, but he did not mind. It had been a long day and the bracing water refreshed the boy. Land was not yet in sight and Cesar continued toward the eastern horizon.

The skiff wobbled over tall swells and came down hard in the troughs, rattling the fishing gear. When the skiff coursed over the biggest swells the Evinrude's propeller lifted entirely out of the water and whined in the air.

The engine sputtered and Cesar reached for the large gas can. It lifted easily. He shut off the Evinrude and unscrewed the caps of both gas cans, and poured the gas in the red can into the larger one. He still saw no land, raising new concern. Absent the Evinrude's calming hum, the wind and waves unsettled the boy and goosebumps rose from his neck to his ankles. He longed to hear his grandfather's voice, to sight land, to see his mother. He longed to be home.

15

Cesar yanked the pull cord and the Evinrude purred. To save gas, the boy attempted to seat the skiff in the swells and to ride them eastward toward the coast, but the swells were swift and the skiff seesawed as they passed beneath the boat. He sought a reassuring glimpse of land. The tiniest peek of the hills would affirm that he would reach the cove in time for dinner.

The offshore wind continued to intensify. Now it blew a constant drizzle of seawater over the boy and his clothes clung to his body. He tugged the drenched rag cap off his head and threw it on the floor of the skiff. With the sun at his back, the water before him was a dull, foreboding blue.

Ahead, Cesar saw flashes of red and yellow. He sat up and saw the colors flash again, followed by a vertical spray of water.

Cesar motored toward the strange visage and saw a curved, compact dorsal fin on top of the wide gunmetal-gray body of a whale, probably a humpback, swimming east. Red and yellow spheres bobbed close to the dorsal fin.

Cesar thought about his grandfather's reverence for the humpback whale, a familiar sight along the Baja. Among the ocean's innumerable creatures, Abuelito reserved his greatest respect for the humpback. It was a good parent to its calves—nurturing, fearless, protective—and it chased the baitfish, just like Cesar and Abuelito. And though a humpback might breech close to the skiff and fill its extensible throat with thousands of tiny fish, it never touched their boat when it fell back into the sea. Abuelito often said the humpback is as gentle as it is big.

Now the humpback whale swam directly in Cesar's path and the boy was surprised to find his skiff closing the distance. The whale dove and Cesar watched the red and yellow spheres follow. The humpback and colored objects quickly resurfaced and lingered on the water.

Cesar drew closer and identified the objects as plastic fishing floats, tethered by plastic rope to blue plastic fishing net that enwrapped the whale from head to dorsal. The fishing net looped through the humpback's long mouth and wound tight around its two blowholes. The tugging action of the floats had sawn a deep groove at the forward base of the whale's dorsal fin, exposing its white blubber, tinged pink with blood.

The humpback kicked its tail, arched and dove. Cesar watched the floats descend until they almost disappeared in the depths, but the exhausted whale immediately resurfaced.

Cesar detected a disjointed movement out of the corner of his eye. He instinctively knew that the source of the movement was neither whale nor wave. He turned and saw a shark, as long as the skiff, swimming along the humpback's side.

Cesar knew the shark's variegated markings well. Abuelito showed him many pictures of tiger sharks and warned his grandson of their rapacious character. Abuelito once crewed for a white boat captain whose beloved companion, an amiable mutt named Presto, was possessed of an inexhaustible enthusiasm for fetch. Abuelito saw a tiger shark pluck Presto like a ripe furry apple when the dog leaped into the sea to retrieve a tennis ball lobbed by a drunken tourist. The captain held the tourist and his two companions at gunpoint with his .22 caliber "shark rifle" while Abuelito bound them with duct tape. The captain recovered the tennis ball and duct-taped it to the drunken tourist's open mouth. "The captives were greatly relieved to see federal police waiting on the dock when we returned to harbor," Abuelito said, "but their mood soured when they learned that the officers had come to arrest them—for what, I do not recall. After a brief negotiation the tourists gave all of their money to the captain and promised they would never to return to the Baja."

The tiger shark shimmied along the humpback's flank and the whale kicked its tail and dove. The floats and shark trailed the whale as it descended. The shark was in no hurry. It would make a leisurely meal of the entangled humpback in a matter of time.

It is because of people, and not the ocean, that this whale is a prisoner of the fishing net, Cesar thought. As a member of the species that created the whale's grim predicament, the boy felt a responsibility. And he felt a duty.

The humpback surfaced and snorted a misty plume that smelled of decay, and the floats sawed the fishing net deeper into the groove on its back. Cesar glanced down at the whale's black eye and observed the same dull luster of resignation that he saw in the caballitos' eyes before he returned them to the sea hours earlier.

On the far side of the humpback the tiger shark rubbed against the whale's body. The spent whale gasped, but this time it did not flinch. And now a second, even longer tiger shark rose from the depths. Scars crisscrossed its pointed snout. Watch this tiger shark well, Cesar thought. It is a fighter.

The sun hung low above the western horizon. Cesar searched for land and saw none. His thoughts wandered to the little cinderblock house where he could be now, comfortable and safe, awaiting his mother's return from the hotel. He longed to tell her about the blue marlin, and his mouth watered at the thought of an amazing meal.

He also thought about Abuelito's words: When a man commits fully to a thing he cannot be stopped.

Cesar grabbed the length of plastic yellow rope off the floor of the skiff and tied one end around the middle bench and the other end around his ankle. He found the fillet knife in the back of the boat and slid it under his belt.

Cesar cut the engine and set the oars in their mounts, and rowed toward the stationary whale, letting the skiff's momentum carry it close. The boy slipped quietly over the side of the skiff into the water so not to frighten the whale or draw the tiger sharks' attention. The deep cold water tensed his body.

He grabbed a handful of net that floated beside the humpback. The whale slapped its tail and flipped the skiff over, spilling its contents across the surface, and dove.

Cesar held on to the fishing net as he submerged. The yellow rope tightened and stretched the boy to the limit of his strength. Seawater filled his eyes and nose. Cesar pulled the knife from his belt with his free hand, reached down and severed the rope.

The humpback resurfaced and drew a ragged breath, its nostril flaps constricted by the fishing net, and Cesar gulped air. He was surprised at the close connection he felt with the whale. He understood this whale, but not like he understood people. He felt the whale's gentle soul.

The humpback arched and dove again, this time a shallow effort that barely pulled the boy underwater. The whale returned to the surface and spouted a faint mist that the wind instantly dissolved.

Cesar clamped the knife between his teeth and pulled himself hand over hand toward the humpback. He scaled the whale's back and crawled toward the red and yellow floats.

A swell washed over the whale and slid the boy across its rubbery flesh. Scattered barnacles tore the boy's T-shirt and raked his chest, and blood oozed from ragged gashes on his skin. Sharp pain and the electric sting of saltwater on his broken skin only focused the boy's resolve.

The tiger sharks kept casual pace with the humpback as Cesar inched his way toward the dorsal fin. When he reached the floats, he removed the knife from his teeth and began cutting away fishing net by the handful.

The scarred tiger shark rocketed out of the water and landed hard on the whale's back, and its tooth-lined jaws chomped at the boy. Cesar swung away from the shark clutching fishing net in one hand and his knife in the other. The whale pitched forward and the boy's legs dragged in water. The shark slid away and Cesar scrambled back up the blue plastic latticework.

Cesar knew that time was running short for the whale. Thank you for your patience, he thought. Just a little more and you will be free to roam the sea, just like me.

Cesar cut away fishing net as fast as his hands would allow. The whale arched and dove. The boy took a deep breath and clutched the net as the humpback descended, but it returned to the surface before he needed another breath of air.

Cesar resumed slicing the fishing net away and felt it loosen. He sawed through another handful of net and the floats drifted free, towing long strands of blue plastic mesh behind them.

The humpback drew a long, deep breath through its unfettered blowholes and dove. With no fishing net to hold onto, Cesar was tossed into the air and landed back-first in the whale's frothing wake. He treaded water and slid the knife into his belt.

Cesar scanned the horizon as he rose and fell with the swells. He glimpsed the red and yellow floats bobbing in the swells and whitecaps a short distance away, and he swam hard toward them.

Now he felt his body's fatigue. His arms cramped and his legs were numbing in the cold open ocean. Whitecaps pummeled the boy as he struggled to straighten his limbs and stretch out painful muscle contractions. The strong westerly wind pushed the floats away faster than Cesar could swim and he made a final desperate effort to reach the plastic spheres, churning the water with stiff arms and legs.

Cesar felt something brush his hand and his stiff fingers hooked the end of a long skein of fishing net attached to the floats. He pulled the floats toward him, choking in the ocean chop.

He glanced back at the receding swells. In the middle distance the humpback breached high in the air and fell back into the sea with a titanic splash.

16

Now the only sound that Cesar heard was the irregular splash of water shaved off the crests of waves by the wind. The sun was setting and the swells were high and spaced far apart. Cesar found footholds in blue fishing net suspended below the floats and rested. He scanned the water for his upturned skiff, but saw no sign of it.

Cesar examined his lacerated chest. Blood seeped from his wounds. He scolded himself for helping the humpback whale. The ocean is vast, he thought. Why would an injured whale be placed in my path? Abuelito said the ocean would provide. Now all it is providing is a pair of plastic floats and no protection from the tiger sharks. Maybe they will follow the whale and forget about me. Or maybe a white boat will find me first, but the sun is low and they will have returned to the harbor by now.

Cesar looked down into the water and saw long strands of blue fishing net dangling beneath the floats like jellyfish tentacles. He felt for his knife, but it had slipped away.

Cesar saw a long shadow pass below his feet. He tried to climb atop the floats, but he rolled back into the water. "Help!" he shouted. The wind blew his parched, panicked cries back in his face.

Cesar closed his eyes and ducked under the water's surface. When he opened them he thought he saw vague forms of tiger sharks circling. He flailed his arms and legs, and pulled himself close to the floats.

The boy's strenuous efforts drained the panic from his body. He pushed his forehead against the red float and closed his eyes. I may be here for a while, he thought. I must protect myself.

Cesar pulled a long strand of fishing net toward him and gathered it under his arm. He tied the end of the strand to the yellow float, creating a long loop. He brought another strand to the red float and tied a second loop. He continued tying loops of fishing net and weaved the loops together.

An hour later he had fashioned a net basket that drooped below the floats. He wrapped himself in the basket and rose and fell with the swells.

The sun was sinking below the horizon and Cesar shuddered, as much with fear as from the persistent chill of the open water. Mama will be home soon, he thought. Maybe Miguel will tell her that I stole the Evinrude and took the skiff. If they discover that Abuelito's fishing gear is also missing they will certainly know that I journeyed far out to sea and they will mount a search. They will find me and I will tell them about the humpback whale—and the blue marlin! Mama will admire my courage! Miguel and Guillermo will be mad with envy! The captains of the white boats will offer me work and mama will insist that I honor Abuelito by crewing on a white boat. I will spend the rest of my life fishing for blue marlin, just like Abuelito.

Cesar gazed west at the soft orange sunset, a beautiful sight to the boy even in his dire predicament. He shivered and his teeth chattered. Darkness would soon be upon him and he fought a mounting fear.

Something bumped the floats and Cesar saw one of the skiff's oars. He threaded the oar through a section of his basket, lifting it even with the surface. Cesar scanned the water for more floating objects. Before night fell he collected several plastic bottles, a Styrofoam boogie board, a length of plastic rope, and a torn hunk from a neoprene wetsuit. He fastened the debris around the rim of his enclosure, raising it even with the surface. He also snagged a sheet of transparent plastic, with which he lined the basket. The ocean is providing, he thought. It is sending me everything I need to survive.

In near-darkness, Cesar felt safe, even relaxed within his plastic cocoon. His body heat warmed the water inside the plastic lining and he no longer shivered. Now his main concerns were hunger and fatigue, and he craved a drink of water. I will eat tomorrow, he thought. The ocean will provide.

Cesar succumbed to his exhaustion. His face fell forward into the seawater, jolting him back to consciousness. He lay his arm on the boogie board and rested his head on his arm, and fell fast asleep.

17

In the middle of the night something in the black water nudged Cesar's elbow. Lost in a deep, distant sleep the boy did not stir. Another nudge opened his eyes. Drifting back to wakefulness, he remembered that he was floating on the open ocean far from land. The wind had died down and the ocean's surface was calm, and thousands of stars shown bright across the dark sky. Cesar scanned the stars for familiar patterns and finding them settled his nerves. In the darkness the bobbing floats were devoid of color. You are poor company, he thought.

His chest wounds burned with each beat of his heart. He traced the swollen cuts with his fingers and fretted that blood might be releasing into the water.

Cesar felt a jet of air on his forearm. He turned and saw a green sea turtle apprising him, its mosaic-tile head resting on the boogie board. The sight of the turtle relaxed the boy for it posed no threat. Green sea turtles used their sharp beaks to scrape algae off rocks and feed on sea grasses, not devour small children. Abuelito admired sea turtles and their peaceful ways. Cesar and his grandfather often paused in their work to watch them go about their happy, unhurried business.

I have no food, but you are welcome to stay, Cesar thought. Tonight you are my guest. Tomorrow we will each find our way home.

The turtle took a breath and slipped off of the boogie board. Please don't leave, turtle, Cesar thought. There is no rush.

Cesar watched the boogie board, but the green sea turtle did not return. Its visit reminded him of his desperate circumstances and he longed for the comforts of home. Mama is looking for me now, he thought. She will send the white boats and they will find me soon. She will prepare a feast when I return and I will tell her about the blue marlin and the humpback whale and the green sea turtle. I will eat three burritos with extra jalapenos and two—no, three—ears of sweet corn. If it pleases her, maybe I will go to school.

Cesar felt safe inside his plastic basket and thoughts of his homecoming eased his fears. He lay his head on his arm and fell off to sleep.

Cesar awakened near dawn. Stars were blinking out and color was returning to the sea. The boy yawned and stretched, forgetting for a moment the wounds on his chest. He hugged his chest and curled in a fetal position until throbbing pain subsided. Cesar longed for a bite of food or sip of fresh water, and he scanned the providing sea for a passing snack.

Several hours later the sky was a deep royal blue to the west and several shades lighter to the east, and the floats glowed red and yellow. Cesar listened for the rumble of white boats. I spotted the floats in rough seas, he thought. The white boats will find them easily in calm morning seas. I will go home soon.

Another hour passed and the sun rose high above the tranquil ocean. Cesar grew impatient. He thought he heard a motor, but he saw only open water in every direction. Again the boy reproached himself for abandoning the safety of his skiff to help the humpback. It is just a whale, he thought. There are many whales in the ocean. If not for one whale I would be home now, asleep in my own bed.

"No, Cesar," he heard Abuelito say. "The life of every living thing is important—no more and no less important than yours. You did what you had to do. You did your duty."

Cesar spun around. "Abuelito?"

The boy saw a sealed plastic food container floating within a few feet of his enclosure. He leaned over the boogie board and reached for the container. He grimaced and his eyes bulged as saltwater stung the wounds on his chest.

Cesar stretched his arm out as far as he could bear and flicked the edge of the container with his fingertips to draw it closer.

The scarred tiger shark exploded out of the water and chomped down on the package. Cesar yanked his hand back and scooted to the far side of the basket.

Twenty feet away a tiger shark's triangular dorsal fin cut the surface. A second dorsal fin appeared and followed. The two tiger sharks circled the boy's enclosure once and slipped beneath the surface. He tracked their direction and waited.

A tiger shark slammed into the back of Cesar's legs. He found himself seated on the shark's snout, his arms and legs akimbo, as it drove the enclosure across the water. The shark veered away and the boy raised his legs to his chest.

Once more a tiger shark struck, penetrating the plastic mesh and ramming into Cesar's chest. The shark shook its head with violent intention and displaced the plastic lining before it withdrew.

Cesar struggled to repair his damaged enclosure and a shark rammed him high on his back. He turned and saw the scarred tiger shark lying on top of the enclosure wall, thrashing its tail to gain entry. The boy cupped his hands over the tiger shark's snout and pushed. The shark rolled away and kicked its tail, splashing a wall of water in Cesar's face.

Cesar held the oar close to his chest like a shield. He felt a jolt and the enclosure dragged across the water. He looked down and saw a tiger shark with fishing net clamped in its jaws, tearing a widening gap. Cesar swallowed saltwater and gasped for air.

The tiger shark released the fishing net and the sheet of transparent plastic floated free. Now all that remained of Cesar's demolished enclosure were the two floats and dangling strands of blue fishing net.

Cesar clung to the floats and felt the bite of cold water. He looked down and saw the two tiger sharks pass through the strands of net. The first shark turned and swam toward the boy. As it approached, Cesar saw crisscrossing scars on its snout.

A chill of terror ran up the boy's spine and his heart lodged in his throat. He drew up his knees and let out a yell, and kicked at the shark as it struck, lifting the boy entirely out of the water.

The sea boiled red. Cesar screamed and kicked with all his strength, and he felt little resistance. He looked down and saw blood curling into the clear water from his shredded right leg, which now ended at his knee.

The boy's blood clouded the water and obscured his view below. Stabbing pain racked his body. His head fell back and he began to black out.

Cesar heard a familiar voice: "Wake up, child. Wake up."

"Abuelito?"

"Wake up, Cesar. You are needed."

Cesar squinted through blood and seawater and saw his grandfather, smiling and radiant, leaning over the bow of a white boat. "You caught the greatest blue marlin in the ocean," Abuelito said. "It is time to go home."

His grandfather's words were a soothing balm. "Home," the boy said in a whisper.

"Hang on, son," a man shouted. An outboard engine gunned and a green inflatable boat pulled alongside the boy. Two men grabbed Cesar's arms and yanked him from the sea, and laid him in on the floor of the inflatable. One of the men looped a band around the boy's torn leg and tied it tight. Cesar looked up at the bow where Abuelito stood, but the bow was empty.

"Home," Cesar whispered. He closed his eyes and drifted away.

18

Cesar awoke from a faraway sleep. His eyes squinted open to a gauzy vision. At first he discerned no detail other than a soft white glow, and he didn't care. An IV drip delivered drugs that numbed the boy and ensured that he would not disturb the sutures that held seams of tucked flesh together below his right thigh.

Cesar surveyed his room. A blank whiteboard hung on a white wall and white linen covered his bed. A clear plastic tube disappeared under a puffy bandage on his left arm. The other end connected to a plastic IV bag that hung from a metal stanchion beside his bed. Clear fluid released into a drip chamber in a soothing cadence. The boy watched the fluid drip, drip, drip, and he sighed with peaceful contentment.

Cesar's eyes widened. The blue marlin crashed his consciousness and flashed its incandescent colors, and now the boy was wide awake.

The images came fast. Cesar saw the blue marlin arc over the skiff and splash into the ocean, and he saw the humpback whale, and the green sea turtle, and—

The boy looked down his bed and cried out. His left foot made a little tent under the sheet at the end of the bed, but his right leg terminated at the knee in a round ball. He struggled to raise himself to his elbows, but the drowsing cocktail of painkillers and sedatives anchored his head to the pillow.

Footsteps clacked across a linoleum floor and two female nurses in white uniforms appeared at the boy's side. One checked an electronic monitor behind his bed. The other inspected his right leg, lifting the sheet at an angle to conceal it from his view. She lowered the sheet and stood over the boy.

"Can you hear me, Cesar?"

"Yes," he said in a weak voice.

"Do you know where you are?"

"A hospital?"

"That's right. Have you been in a hospital before?"

"No."

"We're happy you chose our hospital for your first visit. We're going to take excellent care of you."

The second nurse stepped away from the monitor. "Do you have any pain?"

"I don't feel anything. Just tired."

"Doctor doesn't want you to feel pain. If you do, will you tell us?"

Cesar nodded. "What day is this?"

"Sunday. You've been with us for nearly three days. You're quite the celebrity. Everyone wants to know what happened to you."

"Is my mama here?"

"She's asleep in the lobby. Shall I get her?"

"Yes."

The second nurse left the room.

"You should try to eat," the other nurse said. "Doctor says you need your nourishment."

"I'm very hungry."

"I'll be right back." The nurse smiled and left the room.

Cesar closed his eyes. He saw the scarred tiger shark push its head through a rent in his plastic enclosure and felt a rush of cold water.

Rosa dashed into the room ahead of the first nurse. Her eyes were red. "Cesar?"

The boy opened his eyes. "I'm fine, mama."

Rosa kissed Cesar's forehead and he felt a teardrop. "My brave son. My brave, brave, son."

"I caught a blue marlin, mama. The biggest you ever saw. I saw Abuelito, too."

Rosa's eyes tightened and she fought back tears. "I am so proud of you. You know I am proud of you, don't you?"

"I'm sorry I didn't tell you—"

"Shhh. It's okay."

The second nurse carried a plastic tray of food into the room. Plastic covers concealed plastic plates. A plastic wrapper contained plastic utensils. Another plastic wrapper held a plastic straw, and a plastic bottle of orange juice lay on its side.

The nurse swung a table over Cesar's bed and set the tray down. She elevated the bed and uncovered the plates. Rosa said, "Look what she brought you, Cesar. A feast."

The second nurse unwrapped the utensils and handed Cesar a spork. "Eat slowly—one bite at a time. And chew your food. Very important."

"What do you do with the plastic?"

"Plastic?"

"All this plastic. There's so much."

"Oh, I'm sure they throw it away somewhere."

"Where?"

"I don't know. Why?"

"Do they throw it in the ocean?"

"You should eat. It will be good for you."

Cesar devoured baked chicken and potatoes, green beans, and lemon-flavored cake, and washed it all down with orange juice. Revitalized by the meal, Cesar told his astounded mother and the nurses about the blue marlin and the humpback whale and the green sea turtle and the tiger sharks. And he told them about the white boat that Abuelito brought to rescue him. At the end of his story the sedatives returned the boy to sleep.

During the next week Cesar recounted his ocean adventure to hospital staff whenever he was asked. With each telling, he augmented his story with previously forgotten details. Only Abuelito's rescue—his story's happy ending—never changed.

As Cesar was weaned off the painkillers and sedatives a steady ache set in, but he tolerated it without complaint. His recovery was much easier than his ordeal at sea.

Cesar's doctor recommended fresh air to hasten his recovery, and a burly male attendant rolled the boy in a wheelchair into the shaded courtyard at the center of the hospital complex.

An old woman with an ashen pallor and sunken eyes sat alone on a bench. A plastic tube wrapped under her nostrils and connected to a portable oxygen tank. An unfiltered cigarette rested between her bony fingers and a long ash smoldered at the end. "You must be the kid who got his leg bit off," the old woman said.

"I am sorry, señora," the attendant said. "Smoking is not permitted on the hospital grounds."

"So call the damn fire department." The old woman took a puff from her cigarette and eyed Cesar. "Tell me about it."

Cesar shared his story with the old woman. Now every detail was clear in his mind and he told it in perfect sequence, with nuance and color and pacing, and concluded on the high note that was Abuelito's rescue.

The old woman smiled faintly and took a long drag. "I believe the part about the shark. The rest you made up."

"That will be enough," the attendant said.

The old woman flicked her burning cigarette on the ground and her eyes narrowed. "Hell's got a special place for little boys who tell big lies." She stood and took the handle of her oxygen tank, and shuffled out of the courtyard.

The attendant waited until the old woman disappeared from view before he wheeled Cesar back to his room. "Don't pay attention to her. She isn't well. She doesn't like much of anything or anybody right now."

No one had questioned Cesar's story and the old

woman's dismissive reaction made him uneasy. "You believe me, don't you?"

"You have to admit, your story is pretty… incredible."

"But you believe me?"

"Doesn't matter what I think, Cesar. I just do my job."

The attendant wheeled the boy into his room. Rosa, his nurses, and his doctor stood around a two-layer chocolate birthday cake with ten burning candles. They burst into a chorus of "Las Mañanitas," the traditional birthday song of Mexico.

This is the morning song that King David used to sing.
Today being the day of your saint, we sing it to you.
Wake up my dearest, wake up, see now that the day has dawned
the sparrows are singing, the moon has finally set.
How lovely is this morning, when I come to greet you
we all come with joy and pleasure to congratulate you.
The very day you were born all the flowers first bloomed
and in the baptismal font all the nightingales sang.
The dawn has come my darling, and the sunlight is here for us.
Rise up and shine with the morning and you'll see that here's the dawn.

Cesar's eyes brightened and the doctor patted the boy's shoulder. "Congratulations, old man," the doctor said. His head was clean-shaven and his smiling eyes peered through wire-rim glasses. "I'm prescribing cake for your recovery. Please eat as much as you can."

Rosa cut slices of cake and passed them around on plastic plates. Cesar gobbled his piece of cake and before he finished his mother handed him another slice. "This is your day, Cesar. You can do anything you want."

"Can I go home?"

"How are you feeling?" the doctor asked.

"I feel good."

"The doctor says you're a fast healer," Rosa said.

The doctor said, "As soon as we're sure your leg is mending properly you can go home. You're very strong. But you have to promise me one thing."

Cesar looked at the doctor. "Yes?"

"Promise me that you won't save any whales or catch any giant marlin until you are fully healed."

Cesar made no reply. After his encounter with the old woman in the courtyard, he wondered if anyone really believed him.

"Reporters have been asking for you," Rosa said. "You should share your story with them."

"I don't know."

"What's the harm? I'll be right there."

"Remember, Cesar—lots of blood." the doctor said. "They like that."

The next morning the attendant wheeled Cesar into the center of a two-camera setup in the hospital lobby. Rosa stood off to the side.

A two-person crew positioned lights and cameras on tripods. Curious visitors gathered behind the cameras and watched.

A young TV reporter wearing a vibrant blue dress

approached. "Hi Cesar, I'm Alicia Salcedo with News 16." Salcedo sat close to the boy. He marveled at her ruby lips and flawless skin. She smiled at his gaze. "Maybe you've seen me. You like News 16?"

"I'm sorry, Alicia, we don't have a TV."

"I know who you are," Rosa said. "I have seen you at the hotel where I work."

"I'll email a link so he can watch his interview on his computer," Salcedo said.

The crew clipped microphones on Cesar and Salcedo, and took positions behind the cameras.

"Ready when you are," a cameraman said.

Bright lights flashed on and Cesar flinched under the glare.

"Whenever you're ready," a cameraman said.

Salcedo introduced Cesar and asked him how his injured leg was healing, and quickly moved to his ocean adventure. Cesar told his story with greater clarity and detail than ever. Salcedo, her crew, and visitors listened with rapt interest. After he recounted Abuelito's rescue, Salcedo turned to the crew. "Got it?"

"Everything."

"Wow," she said. "Thank you so much, Cesar. Is this your first interview?"

"Yes."

"You're a natural. We won't have to edit anything. The piece will air tonight."

"Can I say one more thing, Alicia?"

"Of course, anything you want." Salcedo glanced at a cameraman.

"Go ahead."

Cesar looked directly into a camera. "The ocean is full of plastic. It's killing whales, fish, turtles and birds. It's killing everything. We throw our plastic trash in the ocean like it's a dump. If we don't stop, the plastic will kill us, too."

"Got it, guys?" Salcedo asked.

"Got it."

"One more thing?" Cesar asked.

Salcedo nodded and the cameraman resumed shooting.

"The ocean provides for us. We must provide for the ocean, too."

Salcedo unclipped her mic. "Of course, Cesar. Lights?" The lights went off.

A visitor standing behind the cameras began clapping and was joined by a dozen onlookers.

"That's a first," Salcedo said to no one in particular.

19

Rosa watched a muted TV that stared down from an upper corner of the hospital room while her son slept. When 16 News came on she awakened the boy and turned up the sound.

At the top of the news Alicia Salcedo teased her interview with Cesar. "Did a boy who miraculously survived a shark attack really save a whale? You'll hear his amazing story tonight."

Rosa glanced at her pensive son. "You're famous, Cesar. The first famous person in our family."

"She didn't believe me."

"Don't be silly. Of course she believed you. Everyone believes you. Why wouldn't they?"

Stories about fires, robberies, a car wreck and a scandal preceded Salcedo's interview, which was edited down to Cesar's encounter with the tiger sharks and made only passing mention of the entangled humpback whale. Omitted were the blue marlin, sea turtle, Abuelito's rescue—and Cesar's warning about plastic in the ocean.

At the close of the segment, Salcedo said, "Cesar's doctor told me that there's no doubt he lost his leg to a shark bite. But whether a young boy left the safety of his little boat to chop fishing net off an entangled whale remains an open question. After all, there are no witnesses to corroborate his extraordinary tale, so all we have is the vivid imagination of a boy. But what an imagination. For 16 News, I'm Alicia Salcedo."

Rosa stabbed the remote at the TV and the screen went black. "That woman is going to get an earful. You did nothing to deserve such disrespectful treatment. She used you."

"She just did her job." Cesar's eyes blinked closed and he fell back to sleep.

After Cesar's interview aired, hordes of media members descended on the hospital to seize a share of the sensational story. Cesar told his story many times and piece by piece his adventure was completely revealed, and heard, read and watched throughout Mexico and beyond. Even his dire warning about the threat of plastic in the ocean was reported in full.

Some skeptical media members pressured Cesar to retract his story. One demanded that he apologize for exaggerating his experience during a live on-camera interview. Rosa drove the reporter away with a withering fusillade of threats and epithets, which was also widely reported. The media was not nearly as intimidating as the tiger sharks and Cesar remained steadfast.

For a time, Cesar's story gripped the nation's attention. His interviews won the biggest TV audiences, sold the most newspapers and magazines, and nearly crashed a few websites, and the media kept the hot story on the front burner. "A Whale of a Tale!" blared one headline.

Public opinion divided into two camps: those who believed the boy and those who did not. The veracity of Cesar's tale was debated in homes, offices, bars and bedrooms. Depending on one's views, personal and professional relationships either strengthened or suffered.

Cards and letters of mixed—and often passionate—sentiment flooded the hospital. Nurses screened Cesar's mail and forwarded only the most supportive and encouraging messages to the boy. The others would not help his recovery.

Among Cesar's greatest supporters were children. They trusted the boy and accepted his story without hesitation. Their messages often included drawings and paintings of sea life described by Cesar. Many depicted him saving a whale, battling a giant blue marlin, or fighting off bloodthirsty sharks. Some even showed Cesar removing plastic from the Baja coast and depositing it in proper receptacles. Occasionally, schoolchildren sent hand-illustrated posters that they created for class projects. The hospital's phones rang off the hook and emails flooded its inbox, and staff was doubled to accommodate the overflow.

Asked for his opinion, the president of Mexico, Raúl Medina, said, "It is my fondest wish that the boy's adventure, as he has described it, has been faithful to the facts. If his story is not accurate, I will look forward to reading the delicious fantasias that he will pen one day." Critics pounced, denouncing Medina as a spineless politician who equivocated on matters of even smallest significance.

One evening a nurse relayed a request from a group of university students with a campus environmental organization that wanted to meet Cesar. His face lit up and he immediately accepted their invitation.

The next day Cesar entered the hospital lobby on crutches at the appointed hour. A half-dozen university students chatted amongst themselves and checked their smartphones. When the students saw Cesar, they rushed to greet the boy.

A petite fresh-faced student introduced herself. "Hi Cesar, I'm Teresa." Her long black hair was tied back in a ponytail.

Carlos, a lanky young man with horn-rimmed glasses and a generous smile, shook the boy's hand firmly. "A lot of people know about plastic pollution now because of you. You've done a great service."

Cesar often thought about the two students that he and Abuelito met at the harbor and now they stood before him. "You gave me and my grandfather some brochures at the harbor near the Tortugas hotel."

Teresa's jaw fell open. "I remember you. That was what, two years ago? You and your grandfather were the only ones who gave us the time of day. Is he here?"

"He died," Cesar said. "But he is near."

"I'm sorry to hear that."

"I remember him well," Carlos said. "We liked your grandfather. He got it."

Cesar smiled and nodded. The students' acknowledgment of Abuelito's concern for the ocean touched the boy's heart.

Teresa said, "We bear gifts." Carlos presented Cesar

with a green T-shirt and crisp orange cap, each printed with logos that read, "Clean Oceans Now." Cesar tugged the oversized shirt over his hospital gown and donned the cap.

"Now you're one of us," Teresa said. "You can never take them off."

A nurse took photos of Cesar and the students with their smart phones.

"Mind if we put your picture on our website and social pages?" Teresa asked.

"Sure," Cesar said, though he did not understand her request.

"People listen to you. Maybe they'll listen to us when they see you on our pages."

"Maybe."

Carlos said, "We hope you'll help us get the word out."

Me, help you? Cesar wondered. I can't even read or write.

"I don't know. I mean, I'd like to help you, but—"

"But what?" Carlos asked. "Is it your leg?"

Teresa said, "You don't have to do anything except tell your story, just like you do on TV."

"I have to go to school."

"No problem," Teresa said. "We'll be your tutors. We're a bunch of mad scientists, but on the smart end of crazy. You'll be hailed as a genius in no time."

Carlos said, "We'd like you to speak to our organization. Maybe we'll pick up a new member or two. We currently have twelve members."

"Thirteen," Teresa said.

"Pedro stopped coming a year ago."

"Twelve."

"If you think it will help," Cesar said.

Carlos scribbled his contact information on a piece of paper and handed it to the boy. "Let me know when you feel up to it."

Cesar stared at the note.

"Do you have email?" Teresa asked.

"For computers?"

"A phone?"

Cesar shrunk with embarrassment. "I don't think they work where I live."

Teresa and Carlos glanced at each other.

"Then we'll just come to your house," Teresa said. "What's your address?"

"I live in the second village south of harbor," Cesar said with a half-grateful, half-apologetic smile. "We're at the end of the road. There's no sign. That's how you'll know it."

"Perfect. See you in a couple weeks. You'll be home by then, right?"

Cesar shrugged. "Hope so."

That night Cesar lay awake in his hospital bed. He wore his orange Clean Oceans Now cap and thought about his new friends. Maybe we can get the plastic out of ocean, he thought.

20

Cesar yearned to return home and fill his lungs with fresh ocean air, far away from sanitizers and disinfectants that stung his nose in the hospital. His doctor told him that he would be fitted with a prosthetic leg in time and thoughts of walking normally again were never far from his mind. The boy practiced walking with one crutch in secret, holding it firmly to his right side and moving it in tandem with his right thigh. Sometimes he unconsciously stepped with his missing right leg and fell, but he always rolled onto his left side to protect his injured leg and scrambled back up before anyone noticed.

Cesar was returning to his room from a practice walk when a nurse raced around a corner and almost bowled him over. "We've been looking everywhere for you," she said, choking out her words. "Jorge Cruz from Universal Television is here. Jorge Cruz, Cesar—and he wants to see you."

Jorge Cruz's broadcasts were watched by a larger percentage of viewers than all of the other leading TV anchors' news programs combined. Cruz had all the tools—a soothing voice, commanding presence, and perhaps most importantly, a dramatic flair that engaged viewers' interest in even his most mundane reports. That he was trim and handsome with wavy black hair and a shock of silver did not harm his ratings, either.

Cesar and the nurse entered the lobby and the boy saw a now-familiar three-camera setup. The lights were already on.

Cruz approached Cesar and the nurse wrung her hands.

"Hello, Cesar, I'm Jorge Cruz."

"I know who you are. I've seen you in my room."

"Mr. Cruz, I'm Alina, Cesar's nurse. I watch you every night. Except for the nights when you aren't on. I watch Cesar, too, of course, so I watch both of you."

Cruz shook Alina's hand and said, "It is my profound pleasure to meet you." Alina flushed and wavered on her feet.

Cruz said to Cesar, "I have something that I think you will be very interested in. Will you please have a seat?"

Cesar sat in one of two chairs that were positioned in front of the cameras. "Mind if we tape?"

"Sure, Jorge. Whenever you're ready to roll."

Cruz smiled. "You're already an old hand at this, Cesar." Camera operators began shooting.

Cruz opened a tablet computer and spoke to the camera. "Last night I received an email from Claudia Hope, who leads an organization in California that disentangles whales from ocean debris. I will read for you now the most interesting part of Claudia's communication:

Like everyone else, we have followed Cesar's story with great interest, though our interest is largely scientific. Two months ago, a humpback whale entangled in fishing net passed along our coast near Santa Barbara. We named the whale, which we believed to be a female, "Grace."

Grace was in a bad way. We tracked her south past San Diego and hoped she might turn around so that we could mount an effort to disentangle her, but Grace continued south along the Baja Peninsula.

After we heard Cesar's story, an alert member of our team took another look at our data. Grace was towing red and yellow fishing floats that matched Cesar's description. She also had a serious wound at the base of her dorsal fin, precisely as described by Cesar.

Yesterday an injured humpback whale was spotted making its way up the coast. The whale reportedly had a deep dorsal wound and we put a team on the water to examine it. We found that the humpback's dorsal injury was healing well. The whale also had markings on its flukes that were distinctive to Grace.

I'm delighted to report that Grace swam with strength and purpose, and we believe she will fully recover. We have no doubt that Cesar's reported encounter with a humpback whale is accurate, and that the whale he said he disentangled off the Baja coast was indeed Grace. We are further convinced that Cesar rescued Grace at a critical time when she might otherwise have perished. We are grateful to Cesar for the enormous personal risk he took to save her life.

Cesar saved a second humpback whale, too. Swimming with Grace was her newborn calf. We're delighted to report that both mother and child are happy and healthy.

Sincerely,

Claudia Hope

Cesar stared at the tablet. "Need a moment?" Cruz asked. Cesar looked at Cruz and smiled.

"Claudia also sent a video that her team shot a few months ago." Cruz played a shaky video on the tablet that showed Grace swimming in choppy seas. Grace breached, and red and yellow floats trailed close behind her dorsal fin.

Cruz looked at the crew. "Cut." The cameras and lights went down. He placed his hand on Cesar's shoulder. "Tonight the world will know the truth."

After Cruz' story aired new waves of media members converged on the hospital to interview the boy and this time none of his words were edited. Alicia Salcedo returned with her 16 News crew and taped a one-hour special report that she titled, "The Young Boy and the Sea." Her report won the second-highest audience ratings that week, after Jorge Cruz's report.

The constant demands of Cesar's celebrity distracted the boy from giving much thought to the long-term implications of his injury. As he adjusted to his daily routine of media interviews, reviewing piles of fan mail, fulfilling autograph requests, and sharing his story with nearly everyone he encountered, his thoughts began to drift back to his dream of crewing on a white boat. Cesar had made good progress in his recovery and he decided to push his doctor for permission to go home.

The doctor listened to Cesar's plea and asked, "Think you can get around without any help?"

"I know I can."

"Let's see two laps."

Cesar and the doctor stood in the long hallway outside the boy's room. Cesar handed the doctor a crutch. "Hold this."

The doctor pushed the crutch back to Cesar. "No unnecessary risks."

Cesar placed the crutch under his arm and loped down the hallway on two crutches without difficulty.

The doctor clapped his hands. "Well done, show-off. Now back."

Cesar leaned a crutch against a wall. "Two crutches," the doctor said. "I would prefer not to perform the same surgery twice."

Cesar disobeyed the doctor's order and crutch-walked back up the hall with long, fluid strides.

"You've been holding out on me," the doctor said.

"I learned how to fall, too. Want to see?"

"That's okay." The doctor removed his glasses and furrowed his brow. "You forgot your other crutch."

Cesar crutch-walked back down the hall and retrieved the second crutch, and used both crutches on his return lap.

The doctor heaved a deep sigh. "It is the considered opinion of this medical professional that you, young man, are uniquely qualified to do just about anything you set your mind to doing, including saving thirty-ton whales. It will be boring around here without you, but if your mother says it's okay, you can go home."

Hospital staff and patients waved as Rosa drove Cesar away in an aging sky-blue Chrysler sedan, purchased with proceeds from the sale of Abuelito's VW bus. Cesar rolled down the passenger window and gulped fresh air. "This car smells worse than the hospital."

Rosa laughed and then they laughed together.

"Miguel saw you on TV. He's been bragging about what good friends you are. He says not to worry about the motor. He even brought us some fish to eat."

Cesar stared out his open window in silence.

"Don't worry about Miguel. I hate that bratty kid, anyway." And they laughed until they ached.

As the miles passed Cesar felt a gathering sense of loss. After his ocean adventure and the excitement at the hospital, Cesar understood that there was a much larger world beyond his village and the harbor. He had travelled over another horizon, discovered new experiences and made new friends. Many of the people he met were highly-educated, conversant in a diverse range of subjects, and often accomplished—some were even famous—and yet they treated Cesar as an equal, with deference and respect, unconcerned about class distinctions that the boy had accepted as an immutable fate of birth.

Before Cesar went to sea to find his destiny, the world outside his village was of little interest to the boy. Now it brimmed with possibilities. Cesar was finally going home, but home would never be the same.

21

After Cesar and his mother returned to the village, the boy slept almost continuously for several days, spent from both his recovery and the incessant demands that accompanied his celebrity. Rosa watched over her son day and night, but tight finances soon compelled her to resume her work at the hotel.

Early one morning Cesar stood in the front doorway of their little house and watched the tail lights of his mother's Chrysler go over the rise. He felt strangely alone, and maybe a little afraid, even though there were no tiger sharks about. A light was on in the Muñoz women's house, but they wouldn't appear for at least a few more hours. Only the gentle rhythm of small waves lapping the coast provided the boy company.

Cesar made his way to the bluff above the cove as the sun rose over the hills. He closed his eyes and took a deep breath, savoring the nourishing sea air.

Cesar looked for the hump of plastic debris that he had piled in the rocks, but wind and waves had erased any trace of it. He gazed west and wondered how far beyond the horizon he had journeyed to catch his blue

marlin; perhaps a distance of two horizons, maybe further.

I will fish again, he thought. First I must do other
work.

22

One Sunday morning Rosa was stirring a simmering pot on the hotplate that would yield the week's meals when a car pulled up. Through the open front door she saw two young people emerge from a white Volvo sedan. Rosa wiped her hands and met them at the door.

Teresa extended her hand. "Hi, Rosa. I'm Teresa and this is Carlos. We've seen you on TV."

Rosa smiled and shook their hands. "Cesar told me about you. Thanks for coming all the way out here."

The annex hatch swung open and Cesar stepped out, leading with his crutch. He wore his green T-shirt and orange cap.

"You give good directions, guy," Teresa said. "We only missed your turn once."

"It's a beautiful day," Rosa said to Cesar. "Why don't you show them around?"

"I don't know what to show you. There isn't much to see."

Teresa nodded toward the ocean. "What's that over there?"

Cesar smiled.

"Show us your most favorite place."

"Follow me." Cesar led Teresa and Carlos toward the bluff.

Rosa said, "I'll have lunch for you when you get back."

Cesar, Teresa and Carlos stood on the bluff and gazed down at the cove. "Stunning," Teresa said. "This is paradise."

Cesar pointed out debris on the beach. "I tried to keep it clean but there is always more plastic. We used to take it to the harbor."

Teresa looked at Carlos. "Maybe we can help."

"Definitely we can help," he said.

Teresa and Carlos hiked down the narrow path to the beach. They collected debris and started a new pile. Cesar sat on the bluff and watched. It pained him to sit idly by while his new friends did all the work.

An hour later Teresa and Carlos rejoined Cesar.

"This is such an amazing spot," Teresa said. "I'm shocked that it hasn't been developed."

"It's only a matter of time," Carlos said. "The hotels are coming this way."

"It would be even better if there was no garbage," Cesar said.

"Unfortunately, the plastic is coming this way, too," Carlos said.

By the time Rosa served dinner Cesar and the two students were fast friends, allied in their mission to cleanse the oceans of plastic pollution. They discussed Cesar's pending visit to the university and Rosa volunteered to drive her son.

Cesar said to Teresa and Carlos, "I don't want to let you down."

Teresa asked, "Let us down? How?"

"I never read your brochures." Cesar looked at his mother, and then the students. "I can't read."

"He plans to go to school," Rosa said. "He's just a little behind."

"Do you really want to learn how to read?" Carlos asked.

"Yes."

"You're going to learn how to read because we're going to teach you," Teresa said. "Mad scientists—remember?"

Cesar smiled and nodded.

The following week Cesar was standing on the bluff when he heard the rumble of an approaching vehicle. He turned and saw a flatbed truck jouncing toward him. Teresa sat behind the wheel, Carlos at her side. Several students stood in back and clutched side panels.

Teresa swung the truck wide at the turnaround and backed toward Cesar. A cloud of dust gathered around the truck when it came to rest. The students piled out and donned gloves.

Carlos handed out large burlap bags. "Alright, people," he said. "Let's collect us some garbage."

The students followed Carlos down the path to the beach in the cove. Cesar ambled after them.

Teresa held a book aloft. "Hold on, cowboy."

Teresa and Cesar sat on the bluff while the students

toted bagfuls of plastic debris from the beach to the flatbed truck. She helped Cesar sound out words in the book. By the time they worked through the last page, the students had removed all visible debris from the cove.

"Enjoy the view," Teresa said. "For at least a week."

"Maybe less than a week."

"Even less than that. The plastic's already there. You're looking at it."

Cesar squinted his eyes. "I don't see any."

"You can't. Nobody can. Plastic breaks down into smaller and smaller pieces until it's too small to see. It's not just killing fish, turtles, mammals and birds. When fish eat or absorb plastic, toxic chemicals enter our food chain. It's only a matter of time before plastic kill us, too—if it isn't already."

Cesar watched the students toss bags of trash into the flatbed truck. "What about the island of plastic? Can it be cleaned up?"

"Of course it can be cleaned up, but only if everyone pitches in. Unfortunately, the Great Pacific Garbage Patch is just the tip of a very large iceberg that extends miles below the surface of the ocean. There's tons more plastic sitting on the bottom, way beyond our reach. And there's more than one garbage patch in the Pacific Ocean. In fact, every ocean has garbage patches. Swirling currents called *gyres* suck the stuff in like giant whirlpools. Millions of tons of plastic debris litter shores around the world, too."

Teresa slapped the book closed and leaned back on her hands.

"Maybe we can't take all the plastic out of the ocean,

but at the very least we have to stop putting it in. People need to learn to reuse stuff. The way things work now is you put soda in a plastic bottle, drink the soda, throw away the bottle. Single use—a global practice that's ruining our oceans and destroying our planet."

"Is that science?"

"Yeah, science. You'll hear a lot of science if you hang out with us."

"So all of you are scientists?"

"Scientists and poets and priests and mothers and fathers and fishermen and lawyers and whale-huggers. We're anybody who cares about what's happening to the oceans."

Cesar watched Carlos carry the last bag of trash up from the cove. "What will you do with the garbage?"

"We'll invite our friends over and throw a big party—beer, wine, music—the works. Just like any swanky party, only with toxic garbage. We'll sort everything into piles—plastic bottles in one pile, plastic bags in another pile, and so on. We'll measure the volume of each pile and take lots of notes. Then we'll sort the plastic by type and measure that, and take more notes. After that, we'll haul the plastic to the recycling center. It's a blast."

"What will you do with your notes?"

"Carlos enters them in his spreadsheet."

"What's that? Like a bed?"

"A very cold bed."

Cesar became pensive and Teresa asked, "What's on your mind?"

"The brochures you gave me and Abuelito—would you mind reading them to me?"

Teresa jumped to her feet. "Let's go." They returned to the house and Cesar retrieved the literature from Abuelito's annex. Teresa, Cesar and Rosa sat at the dining table and Teresa read the brochures out loud. She read that plastic waste impacts people in every society. Much of the plastic debris in the oceans originates from developing countries that struggle to manage their plastic waste. As a result, it may be discarded in lagoons, streams and rivers that empty into the ocean. She read that developed countries are also careless with plastic, manufacturing more plastic products each year, while recycling only a tiny fraction of it. She looked at Cesar and said that ten percent of plastic in the oceans originates from boats.

Teresa set the brochures down.

Rosa sighed. "Is there any good news?"

"Organizations like Clean Oceans Now are working hard to eradicate plastic pollution, so that's good news. Some of us are focused on collecting plastic debris in the ocean and others are collecting it on the shore. Others are trying to build floating recycling factories. Biodegradable bioplastics made from renewable resources may eventually replace petrochemical and synthetic plastics. We can all do better with the way we use plastic, whether it's reusing plastic that we already have or just buying less of the stuff. Unfortunately, many people aren't even aware that there is problem."

Cesar felt a weighty burden of responsibility. "I haven't done enough."

Teresa reached across the table and touched the boy's hand. "We're all responsible."

Carlos poked his head in the half-open door. "Knock, knock." He and the other students stepped inside.

Rosa got up from the table and handed out drinking glasses. She removed a pitcher of cold water from the refrigerator and filled everyone's glass.

"Knowledge is power," Teresa said. "People need to be educated. If they knew how much harm that plastic is doing, they would change their ways."

"First, we have to reduce our consumption," Carlos said. "That means using fewer plastic bags and more reusable bags, and avoiding disposable and single-use products such as water bottles and cosmetics packaging. Do toys have to be plastic? Can we live without plastic razors or those plastic dental floss things? There are good alternatives. When we do use plastic, we need to recycle it." Carlos held up his glass. "We're all in this together, right?"

Everyone clinked glasses.

After the students departed, Rosa was drying dishes when Cesar set Teresa's book on the table. He opened the book to the first page and began reading, sounding out each word with utmost care. "How I wish I was a fish, alive and free, beneath the sea."

Rosa's eyes watered. "Teresa gave you that?"

Cesar nodded.

"I have never heard such beautiful words."

23

Before he spoke at the university, Cesar and his mother toured the campus with Teresa and Carlos. They strolled through a metal-and-glass library that had more computers than books, then circled a massive soccer stadium, open at one end, and watched the women's soccer team practice on green plastic turf. Later, they stood in the back of an expansive theater and watched the dress rehearsal for a Shakespeare play. All across the campus Cesar saw students studying, debating and hustling to classes.

Cesar decided that this day was as wondrous as any he had spent on the ocean, save for the day he caught his blue marlin. The university is as colorful and diverse as the fish in the sea, he thought. He wanted to be a part of it.

Teresa asked Carlos, "Do we have time for a quick bite?"

Cesar and Rosa hadn't eaten since early that morning, but held their tongues as a courtesy to their hosts.

"The doors are already open," Carlos said. "Someone might be waiting."

Teresa said to Cesar and Rosa, "You must be starving."

Cesar showed no reaction. "A little snack might be nice," Rosa said.

Teresa said to Carlos, "We'll just have to be fashionably late."

"Fashionably late is still late."

Teresa stared at Carlos.

"Late it shall be," he said.

They entered a near-empty dining hall and pushed trays along a buffet rail, selecting food and beverages from refrigerated cases.

Teresa placed a slice of pie in a plastic container on her tray.

Carlos said to Cesar, "You'll love the pie. Try the cherry."

Instead, Cesar selected a banana, an apple, and a cardboard carton of chocolate milk with no straw.

Teresa eyed Cesar's odd serving. "No sandwich? Not even a cookie? You must be hungrier than that."

"Cesar swore off plastic packaging," Rosa said. "He feels bad about all the plastic he used in the hospital."

"Everything was wrapped in plastic," Cesar said. "They took full bags of plastic out of my room twice a day. Plastic bags full of plastic."

Teresa walked back down the buffet and placed her piece of pie back in the refrigerated case.

Carlos shook his head and returned his plastic-wrapped sandwich to another case, and picked an apple out of a bowl.

On their way out of the dining hall, Teresa reached

into a trash receptacle and pulled out an empty plastic water bottle.

Cesar's group crossed a quad and approached a conference room where a crush of students, teachers and administrators milled around open double doors. When Carlos saw the mob, he combed his fingers through his hair and said, "Unbelievable."

Carlos announced Cesar's arrival at the door. "Make room, people. Coming through." The crowd parted when they saw the boy.

Inside, attendees stood along the walls and filled every chair. They thrust pens and papers into Cesar's hands as he passed, and he stopped and posed for many selfies.

Cesar, Rosa and Teresa arrived at the front of the room. The boisterous audience broke into a chant— "Cesar! Cesar! Cesar!"—clapping and stomping their feet in time with their chant. The boy bowed his head and looked away. Teresa stepped to a lectern and took a deep preparatory breath, then spoke into a microphone. "Thank you all for coming."

Applause and cheers continued. Teresa moved away from the lectern and joined the delirium. After a few minutes the audience quieted. Teresa returned to the lectern and spoke.

"Cesar came a long way today to share his amazing story of survival. That's why most of us are here. But he's also going to talk about this." Teresa held up the empty plastic bottle that she retrieved in the dining hall. "Cesar has spent most of his young life on the ocean, probably more time than all of us combined. A couple years ago we visited the harbor where Cesar and his grandfather kept their fishing boat. We handed out literature and talked to fishermen about plastic pollution. Cesar and his grandfather cared enough to try to do something about it. Every time they fished they brought plastic debris that they found in the water back to shore. They made a difference."

The audience applauded politely.

"See this innocent-looking plastic bottle?" Teresa examined the bottle as if it was some rare and wondrous thing. "Today somebody drank water out of it—maybe one of us—then threw the empty bottle in the trash.

"This handful of plastic will probably end up in a dump, where it will slowly break down, year after year, decade after decade, for centuries to come. And so what? Out of sight, out of mind, right? In the ocean, plastic breaks down into confetti-sized pieces that fish and marine mammals mistake for food. When they fill their bellies with those tiny bits of plastic, it ruptures their intestines or starves them to death. Toxic chemicals in the plastic get into the fish, and then we eat the fish. The chemicals have been linked to all kinds of bad stuff— cancer, birth defects, infertility. Plastic isn't good for turtles, isn't good for birds, isn't good for whales, isn't good for fish—and it sure isn't good for us."

Teresa set the empty plastic bottle on the lectern.

"In the old days you had to build a pyramid or compose a brilliant symphony to leave your mark. Now you just drink a bottle of water and throw away the empty, and there's your legacy. That bottle will still be around long after you, your children, their children, and lots of marine species that it choked, starved or poisoned have left the stage. This plastic bottle, plus the other ten thousand pieces of plastic that you'll throw away during your lifetime, could be your legacy. Question is, do you want it to be? Not me."

The audience murmured and the air grew stale. Teresa sensed a mounting unease with her litany of plastic horrors.

She glanced back at Cesar. "We are fortunate that one courageous boy brought the problem of plastic pollution to the attention of millions of people who didn't have a clue about it. Cesar's amazing story of survival has given him a platform to share how plastic is clogging our waterways, poisoning our oceans, torturing marine life, and maybe even killing us. After he's done speaking, please stop by the Clean Oceans Now table at the back of the room if you'd like to help us get plastic out of the ocean. Now for the fun part. Give it up for Cesar."

The audience stood and cheered. Teresa slid a wooden box against the base of the lectern and adjusted the mic. Cesar stepped on the box and spoke into the microphone. "Hello?" The boy's voice boomed into the room from high above. He searched the ceiling for the source of the sound.

Cesar gazed at the sea of expectant faces. He was accustomed to sitting for media interviews that would later be viewed by many thousands of people, but not appearing live before hundreds of gawking eyes all at once. Just tell my story, he thought. Tell it exactly as it happened and everything will be okay.

Cesar launched into his story. He included his and

Abuelito's plastic clean-up practices on the ocean and on the beaches, and added his observations about the plastic packaging he saw in the hospital and dining hall.

At the conclusion of his talk Cesar shared his plan to study science and help remove plastic from the ocean permanently. "The ocean has provided for us. Now we must provide for the ocean. It is our duty."

The audience rose and applauded, and gathered around the boy for more autographs and photos.

Cesar and Rosa made their way through the throng toward the exit. Attendees stood three-deep around the Clean Oceans Now table, where Teresa had joined Carlos to sign up new volunteers. A paper banner emblazoned with the organization's name hung on the wall behind them.

Cesar and Rosa watched for a while and then slipped out the door.

24

The sun was still high when Cesar and Rosa drove away from the campus. "The hospital isn't very far," Rosa said. "We have time if you want to stop by."

"Let's go." Cesar made many friends among the patients and staff. He hoped to see them again.

Rosa parked the Chrysler in the patient loading zone by the hospital entrance and entered the lobby with Cesar. Nurses and staff were delighted to see the boy and greeted him like an old friend. Rosa whispered to a hospital staffer, "He spoke at the university today. Hundreds of people came to hear him."

A nurse presented several bundles of letters and postcards to Cesar, and handed a sticky note scrawled with a phone number to Rosa. "The president's office called. Three times."

"What president?" asked Rosa.

"*The* president. President Medina."

Rosa caught her breath. "We don't have a phone just now. We plan to get one."

"I insist you use ours," the nurse said. "We're dying

to find out what they want."

The nurse sat Cesar and Rosa behind the reception desk and picked up the phone. "Ready?"

Cesar and his mother nodded. The nurse dialed and handed the phone to Cesar when she heard a ring. The boy held the receiver tight to his ear.

"My name is Cesar and I have a message to call you…Cesar…Yes, I have a message to call."

He looked at his mother and shrugged, and handed her the phone.

"Hello? I am Cesar's mother. Somebody called my son at the hospital where he stayed…Yes, a big shark…No, bigger than that...Yes, a tiger shark." Rosa handed the phone back to Cesar. "She said to wait."

Cesar listened and heard a voice. "Yes, this is Cesar…Hello, Raúl…Thank you, Raúl. It's nice to meet you, too." Nurses and attendants looked at each other and gasped. "It would be nice to visit you. Can my mama come?...Okay, I'll get her." Cesar handed the phone to his mother. "Raúl is getting his assistant."

The reception desk spectators whispered and nudged each other. A voice came on the other end of the line.

"I'm Cesar's mother…He would be thrilled to meet President Medina…We live a very long way from Mexico City…Where did you say?"

Rosa held her hand over the mouthpiece and said to the nurse, "Will you write this down?" The nurse grabbed a pen.

Rosa said, "Saturday, 10 a.m., La Costa Airport." The nurse scribbled the information on the back of an envelope.

"Yes, I can find it...Okay, see you on Saturday."

Rosa hung up the phone and touched her fingers to her lips. "I need a dress."

"Well? What did they say?" the nurse asked.

"We're going to meet President Medina. He's sending his helicopter." Rosa smiled at her son. "A helicopter, Cesar. How about that?"

"Why?"

The nurse took the boy's hand. "Because you are a hero."

Cesar frowned. "I am not a hero."

Rosa kneeled by her son. "Do you want to tell people about the plastic?"

Cesar smiled. "Yes."

On Saturday morning Rosa and Cesar drove to La Costa Airport, a single-strip gravel runway with a one-room cinderblock terminal perched atop a shaved-off mountain. A frayed, faded windsock hung limp on a pole above the building. Parked on one side of the terminal were two single-prop aircraft and a rusty tractor was hitched to an even rustier land-leveler.

Rosa backed her Chrysler next to the tractor. After a closer inspection of the ancient machine she decided that parking her car on the opposite side of the terminal would improve its appearance.

Cesar and Rosa stepped out of the Chrysler into blazing sunshine and walked to the terminal door. Cesar wore his orange Clean Oceans Now cap, a light blue cotton shirt and baggy black slacks—right pant leg pinned up—which would fit for a few more years. His grandfather's vintage red-and-brown scallop-patterned necktie hung from his neck. Rosa wore a simple white cotton dress and an extra layer of makeup.

Cesar tried to turn the doorknob, but it was locked. The boy and his mother retreated to the Chrysler, which had no air conditioning and was now in a sweltering condition.

Rosa fussed with her makeup in the car's rearview mirror. After thirty minutes they hadn't seen a soul, only a big jackrabbit that scampered across the runway in a futile attempt to escape the blistering sun.

Rosa wondered why the president of Mexico would dispatch his helicopter to such an unseemly place to pick up two people who had nothing to do with the fate of the country, and never would. Maybe it was all just a hoax. The thought made her temperature rise even higher.

Cesar was the first to hear the chop of rotor blades. He stepped out of the Chrysler and gazed south.

A wide-bodied helicopter suspended beneath the metallic blur of spinning rotors approached the airstrip at a low altitude. Red and green stripes ran the length of the bulky white fuselage.

Relieved by the helicopter's arrival, Rosa stepped to her son's side and put her arm around his shoulder. "You make me so proud."

The helicopter's rotor blades swept up an expanding cloud of dust. Cesar and Rosa closed their eyes and pursed their lips, and stood fast against a swirling spray of dirt and sand.

The helicopter touched down and reduced rotor

speed. Cesar and his mother opened their grit-encrusted eyelids. Dust clung to their hair and clothes. Rosa's face, tacky with sweat and makeup, wore a velvety mask of grime. Cesar removed his cap and beat away the dust against his crutch.

The helicopter door swung open and a stairway unfolded. A prim woman in a blue uniform stepped down the stairs and staggered across the airstrip in high heels. She extended her hand and said, "I'm Graciella Martinez," then stumbled and fell into Rosa's arms. "I'm terribly sorry," Martinez said, regaining her balance and composure.

Rosa opened her mouth and fractured her monotone mask of dirt. "We are honored to meet you." She squeezed her son's arm. "Aren't we?"

"Honored."

"President Medina is looking forward to meeting you, too. This way, please."

Martinez trudged back to the helicopter and Cesar and Rosa followed. Martinez stopped at the bottom of the stairs and asked Cesar, "Have you ridden in a helicopter?" Cesar shook his head and clambered into the air-conditioned transport.

Cesar and his mother settled into tall black leather seats opposite Martinez. "It's nice and cool in here," Rosa said with a delighted sigh. A crew member closed the door and the helicopter lifted off.

Cesar stared out the window and gripped his armrests tight. Rosa opened a compact and gulped when she looked in the mirror. Martinez produced a packet of facial wipes and handed it to Rosa. "For just such emergencies." Rosa handed a wipe to Cesar and went about mopping her face.

"What's your size and color?" Martinez asked. "I'll order a clean dress for you and a nice suit for Cesar. You'll be picture-perfect." Rosa provided measurements and Martinez called ahead.

The helicopter flew south along the western Baja coast. Cesar was glued to the window, studying hills, dunes, lagoons, roads, harbors and variations in the ocean's surface. The boy imagined that his blue marlin was swimming somewhere in the water below. He wondered about the lives of inhabitants in the tiny fishing villages he saw, and if there might be other boys like him.

At the southern tip of the Baja, the helicopter flew over hilltop villas and resorts, and banked east over jutting rock formations, around which catamarans, sailboats, motorboats, double-decker cruisers and yachts were crowded with tourists who wore colorful hats, T-shirts and swim attire. "Cabo San Lucas," Martinez said. "The president comes here to relax with his family."

The helicopter veered over a bay lined with a wide beach and more resorts, and continued west above a harbor filled with the biggest white boats Cesar had ever seen.

The aircraft descended toward a whitewashed villa with a red terracotta-tile roof high on the western edge of a craggy ridge. It put down on a circular concrete pad marked with a big yellow "X." A dozen black SUVs with tinted windows were parked on a broad driveway near the pad.

The helicopter rotors slowed and stopped. A man in

a dark suit strode to the door and opened it. Martinez stepped down the helicopter's stairs. Cesar and Rosa paused at the door and took in the majestic view. The Pacific Ocean stretched for miles before them.

A young woman wearing a festive floral dress approached. "Welcome," she said. "The president is looking forward to meeting you. My name is Elena. Please come with me."

Cesar and Rosa followed Elena into the villa. They passed two more men in dark suits and entered a bedroom that was larger than their entire house. The bedroom had wide sliding glass doors, a boveda ceiling, and two king beds with ruffled white bedspreads. A black suit, Cesar's size, lay on one bed and an emerald green dress on the other. "I hope you like your clothes," Elena said.

"They're beautiful," Rosa said. "And the beds—I have never seen such linens."

"You're welcome to take the clothes with you, but you'll probably have to leave the bedding," Elena said with a laugh. "I'll get a bag for your soiled things. The bathroom is over there. See you in an hour."

Elena left the room and closed the door. Rosa picked up the dress and held it to her nose, inhaling the fabric like a fragrant flower bouquet. "I just want to eat this dress. Maybe I will."

Cesar walked to the bed where his suit lay. A crisp white shirt was folded inside the jacket and a shiny red necktie lay on top of the shirt.

He walked to a sliding glass door and looked out at the ocean. He imagined that Abuelito was sitting in the skiff far out on the water, looking back at the villa, waving. The boy smiled at the thought.

25

An hour later Elena showed Cesar and Rosa into an expansive living room with a soaring unfinished-wood ceiling. Big bouquets of flowers were arranged around the room.

A wall of sliding glass doors opened to a sprawling patio and lawn, and crisp ocean air filled the room. Outside, men in dark suits and sunglasses walked the property.

Cesar and Rosa sat on one of three white sectional sofas.

"Something to drink or nibble on?" Elena asked.

Cesar started to speak and Rosa said, "Anything will be fine." Elena disappeared down a hallway.

A moment later President Medina strode into the room with his coifed, elegant wife, Lucia, and three children, all near Cesar's age—Héctor and Javiér, both slim and serious, and their younger sister, Maribel, who wore a bright, carefree smile. The barrel-chested president was attired in cream-colored slacks and an untucked tangerine shirt. Cesar and Rosa scrambled to their feet. "Welcome to my home," Medina said in a booming voice that filled the enormous room. "I am so happy you came."

"It is an honor to meet you, President Medina," Rosa said.

"It is an honor," Cesar said.

"Please—just Raúl. This is my wife, Lucia, and my children, Maribel, Javiér and Héctor. Cesar, you recently turned ten, no?"

"Yes."

"Héctor is nine and Javiér is ten. You have much in common."

A photographer carried a hefty black camera into the room. Medina clamped a beefy hand on Cesar's shoulder. "Mind if we take a few photos for the press?"

"Sure, Raúl."

President Medina and Cesar stood close together and smiled, and the photographer clicked away. "I confess that I did not always believe your story, Cesar, for which I am truly sorry. It got me into hot water with many people, some of whom, I am ashamed to admit, include members of my own family. I pledge to you that I will work hard to correct the record."

"That's okay, Raúl. I have made worse mistakes."

Elena rolled a cart arrayed with iced tea, juice and soda into the room. Drinks were served and everyone spread out on one of the sofas.

"So how is your leg?" the president asked. "Are you having much pain?"

"It's fine, Raúl. Better every day."

"That's what I thought you would say. You're a very strong boy."

"He never complains," Rosa said. "That's how he

was raised."

"I was told about your father, Rosa. I am sorry for your loss."

"Thank you, Raúl. We are doing well."

Héctor leaned toward Cesar. "Tell us about the sharks."

"He has told his story many times," Lucia Medina said. She looked at Cesar. "You must weary of it."

"You've heard Cesar's story before, Héctor," President Medina said. "He didn't come all this way to tell it again."

"I don't mind," said Cesar.

"Tell us," Maribel said. "Please."

"Don't leave anything out," Javiér said. "Especially the sharks."

Lucia glowered at her son. "Javiér."

Cesar shared his story with the Medina family and omitted not a single detail. He started his story with Teresa's and Carlos' visit to the harbor and learning about the island of plastic in the middle of the ocean. When he reached the part about scraping his chest on the humpback's barnacles, Javiér said, "Let me see."

"Javiér, please," Lucia said. "My sons can be impulsive," she said to Rosa, "just like their father."

"That's okay." Cesar unbuttoned his shirt and pulled it open. Fresh pink scars lined his chest. Héctor and Maribel winced and looked away. Javiér gaped at the marks. "Awesome," he said with no small envy.

Cesar told the Medina family that plastic in the ocean was killing fish and wildlife, and he explained how it threatened people, too. He spoke of his and his grandfa-

151

ther's efforts to remove plastic from the sea. "We took many buckets of plastic away, but no matter how many buckets we took, there was always more."

The Medina family fell into vexed silence, the romance of Cesar's ocean saga dimmed by the gloomy plastic predicament.

Rosa said, "It's just something he thinks about, that's all."

"What would you propose to do about this plastic problem?" the president asked.

Cesar massaged his right thigh and contemplated the question. "Abuelito and I didn't know about it until Teresa and Carlos told us. Most people don't know about it. If they did, I am certain that they would make changes. If everyone makes changes, things will be different."

"We use plastic for everything," Medina said. "Businesses and manufacturers need plastic. Doctors, plumbers—everyone needs plastic. We can't just snap our fingers and make it go away."

"When I was in the hospital all of my food was wrapped in plastic. I had no choice. Now I am out of the hospital and I no longer eat food that is contained in plastic. I'm not starving. We must find a way. It is our duty."

Medina pursed his lips and glanced toward the ocean. "More than a few of my critics contend that I don't care about the natural environment. I would like nothing more than to subdue one of their more persistent lines of attack. But if I change my policies, I might make even more enemies—especially within my own party. On the other hand, my poll numbers might improve. The election is coming and my numbers are not where they need to be. That is also something to consider."

"What do you want, Raúl?" Lucia asked. "What would you do if the politics didn't matter?"

"What do I want?" Medina's face sagged. He looked into his glass and swirled the ice. "I have not considered that question for a very long time."

"When we were students we had no money for nice restaurants and hotels," Lucia said to her husband. "We slept on the beach and we were never happier. We dreamed of impossible things, and look—they came true. Have we forgotten how to dream?"

Elena rolled another cart into the room and served sandwiches and snacks.

The president asked Cesar, "Is there anything you would like to see while you're here?"

"I saw many white boats in the harbor. I would like to see them."

"'White boats?'"

"That's what he calls the big fiberglass boats," Rosa said.

Medina nodded. "Of course—white boats. I have a very special white boat, Cesar. Would you like to see my white boat?"

"I would like that very much, Raúl."

Medina turned to Elena. "Please make arrangements." Elena dialed her smart phone and left the room.

A short while later, a caravan of federal police vehicles led a tight formation of black SUVs into the harbor parking lot. Dozens of security staff dispersed around the largest boat, a luxurious three-decker yacht. A Mexican flag swayed over the fly bridge.

Cesar and Rosa followed the Medina family and a retinue of aides and security personnel up a ramp and boarded the yacht. Uniformed crew made preparations and the yacht pulled away from the dock and motored into the bay, followed by several smaller craft that carried security teams.

Rosa sat with Lucia and Raúl Medina on the sundeck and sipped lemonade while Cesar toured the yacht with the president's children. The boy saw a grand salon, state-of-the-art media room, posh staterooms, and several kitchens, and learned about the yacht's famous guests, including movie stars, athletes and dignitaries. Cesar listened politely, but he did not recognize a single name.

In the dining room, Cesar played a shuffleboard game improvised by the Medina children. They sprinkled salt on a long mahogany table and slid plastic coasters bearing the presidential seal from one end to the other.

At the end of the game Cesar asked a passing housekeeper, "Do you have a vacuum?" The housekeeper nodded. She wore a white uniform similar to his mother's hotel outfit.

"May I borrow it?"

The housekeeper went into a hallway and returned with a vacuum. Cesar plugged it into a wall socket and vacuumed salt off the table, chairs and carpeted floor.

"That's her job," Javiér said.

"It's my mama's job, too," Cesar said.

Maribel said, "I want to vacuum."

Héctor took the vacuum from Cesar. "Me first."

All four children took turns with the vacuum before

the last granule of salt was cleaned up. The Medina children treasured their moments with the machine, passing it along to its next custodian with severe reluctance.

"Should we show him?" Javiér asked Héctor and Maribel. The siblings whispered and nodded. Javiér turned to Cesar. "Can you be trusted?"

"Yes," Cesar said, and the Evinrude flashed in his mind. I didn't steal it, he thought. I fixed a mistake.

The Medina children led Cesar through a large commercial-grade kitchen and along a narrow catwalk in the engine room. In the bow below the staterooms, Héctor opened a compartment door and crawled into the dark space. A flashlight flicked on inside and the other three children entered.

Javiér closed the door and two more flashlights came on. The compact space was stuffed with cushions, snacks, comic books, and glittery treasures appropriated by the Medina children from the upper decks. Héctor and Javiér leaned against pillows that lined the slanted hull.

Cesar was taken with a glass paperweight embedded with lifelike oceanic flora and fauna, and he examined it closely. The Medina children trained their flashlights on the colorful paperweight and it glowed in Cesar's hands. "You want it?" Héctor asked.

"Thank you, but I would have no use for it."

"You don't use it," Javiér said. "You just look at it."

"A pri-minister gave it to papa," Maribel said. "Everybody gives things to each other."

"No thank you."

Héctor said, "Now that we've shown you our private

quarters, you must contribute something."

Cesar considered his boxes of sporting goods and his spare crutch, but he possessed nothing so grand as the paperweight.

Maribel said, "It can be anything, Cesar. It just has to be good."

Cesar took off his Clean Oceans Now cap and gave it a long, last look.

Before Cesar offered his cap, Héctor said, "We accept your gift."

On the sundeck, Lucia summoned Elena. "Where are the kids?"

"In their hiding place in the bow."

Lucia said to Rosa, "The kids found a cozy spot where they can get away from it all. It can be lonely for children to be dragged to stuffy events, constantly dressing up for the cameras, spending their free time with self-important adults. We're happy they can find some privacy and just be themselves."

"They're very generous with our property," President Medina said. "They may offer a present to your son."

"Don't worry," Rosa said, "he won't accept it."

"It's fine," Lucia said. "We give the children lots of latitude."

"We've accumulated more stuff than we'll ever need," the president said. "I don't know where half of it came from."

Rosa's shoulders straightened. "Just the same, he won't take it. That's just how he was raised."

"Cesar is quite remarkable," Lucia said. "I can only

hope that my children will be as resilient and high-minded as your son. If I ask Javiér to do something he doesn't want to do, he may fall ill for a week."

"His grandfather deserves much credit," Rosa said. "They were inseparable. Maybe they still are."

The yacht cruised toward the serrated pinnacles at land's end and the children joined their parents on the sundeck. A crew member gave Cesar and Rosa caps emblazoned with "The Lucia" and two hooded raincoats.

"Something to remember your visit," President Medina said.

Rosa looked skyward. "Thank you, but I don't think it's going to rain."

Lucia said, "I'll let you in on a little fashion secret—they protect beautiful hair and pretty clothes from heedless helicopters."

Rosa folded the raincoat and placed it and the other raincoat on her lap. "We'll take them."

The yacht rounded jagged spires and a wide arch formation. At its base, a colony of sea lions barked and sunned on a narrow beach. Passengers on various leisure craft waved and snapped pictures of the presidential yacht. Some made rude gestures and shouted vicious denunciations too far away to be heard. They reminded Cesar of Guillermo and the drivers who sped around Abuelito's VW bus.

"The sea is one of our great heritages," President Medina said. "We have a moral and historic obligation to preserve it for future generations. Isn't that right, Cesar?"

"That's right, Raúl."

Lucia and her children gazed at the president.

"I have given the plastic question some thought," he said. "It's a big problem, bigger than I imagined. I can't fix it by myself. Would you help me?"

"I will do anything you ask. I know others who will also help."

"Young people have not been my biggest supporters. Do you think they would listen to me?"

"They will listen to me."

Javiér raised his hand. "I want to help."

"Me too," Maribel and Héctor said.

Lucia placed her hand on her chest and laughed. "Oh, my. These can't be my children."

"You might have a future in politics, Cesar," the president said. "I can't get them to clean the pool and now they want to clean the ocean."

Medina stood. "We will do good work together." He extended his hand and Cesar shook it firmly. "Mind you, it will be hard work."

Rosa cocked her head. "Nobody works harder than my son."

"We would be a more effective team if you lived closer to my offices."

"Cesar has a private tutor," Rosa said with a whiff of pride. "He plans to attend school."

"My sons attend a private academy. Would you consider enrolling your son?"

"I'm sorry, it is beyond our means."

"If I secure a scholarship for the boy? I will find work for you, too. Whatever you like."

Rosa glanced at Cesar and back at Medina. "Cesar loves the ocean. It is his ambition to work on a white boat."

"And learn science," Cesar said.

"If you want to work on a white boat, Cesar, I insist you work on mine," Medina said. "You can study with your tutors whenever you wish. Rosa, you must also come and work on my boat. Will you do that?"

"Can Cesar live at our house?" Maribel asked.

"We have plenty of places for them to live," Lucia said. She looked at Rosa and said, "We own many properties. You can have your pick."

Rosa caught her breath. "You are so generous. I don't know what to say."

President Medina said, "Discuss it and let me know your wishes."

"Come to the academy, Cesar," Héctor said. "I'll introduce you to all my friends."

"We will all help you with the plastic," Javiér said.

President Medina said, "We can't let plastic pollution ruin the ocean for our children and future generations."

"No, we can't," Cesar said.

"And we won't."

26

A few days later, Cesar was sitting in front of his house reading his book when Teresa and Carlos drove up.

Teresa stepped out of the car. "We need to get you a phone, guy."

Carlos laid a newspaper on the hood of Rosa's Chrysler. The front page showed a large photo of Cesar with President Medina. "You've been busy."

"What does it say?"

Teresa said, "The headline reads, 'President Medina Announces Public Education Initiative to Address Marine Pollution.' The caption reads, 'Boy-hero who saved a whale and survived a shark attack will serve as honorary ambassador.' So now you're a hero and an ambassador. Impressive."

Carlos shook his head. "Unbelievable."

"When did this happen?" Teresa asked. "We just saw you like, what, last week?"

"Raúl flew us—"

Carlos' mouth fell open. "'Raúl?'"

"'Flew us?'" Teresa said.

"He flew us to his house in his helicopter. I told him about you. He needs your help."

Carlos gaped at Teresa. "Raúl Medina needs our help. That's a laugh."

Rosa emerged from the house and Teresa gave her a hug. Rosa looked over Teresa's shoulder and saw the newspaper lying on the Chrysler. "Cesar, you're in the papers."

Carlos' eyes tightened. "Raúl Medina is in the back pocket of some of the biggest polluters in the world. What's his angle?"

"He's very sincere about working with you," Rosa said.

"Carlos isn't a big fan of President Medina," Teresa said. "Fact is, I'm not either."

"He'll exploit Cesar for his own selfish purposes," Carlos said. "That's what guys like him do. That's how they get elected."

"And rich," Teresa said.

"Don't be so sure," Rosa said. "Talk to him. Then decide."

Teresa folded her arms. "Think about it, Carlos. We educated Cesar and his grandfather about plastic, Cesar educated the president, and now the president wants to educate the whole country. This is exactly why we started Clean Oceans Now."

"Come on, Teresa. We've worked too hard to build a reputation for integrity."

"Before Cesar showed up, Clean Oceans Now was on life support," Teresa said. "So we have integrity. So what?"

Carlos looked down and frowned at his industrial hemp shoes.

"You should at least talk to the guy," Teresa said. "You need more data."

Carlos looked up and his face brightened. "You're right. I need more data. I don't have enough data."

"Let's call Raúl," Cesar said.

Carlos smiled and nodded. "Raúl. Unbelievable."

27

That night the rasp of churning dirt and stone awakened Cesar. The headlights of a passing vehicle set his floral curtains aglow before it moved on and returned his bedroom to near-black. Cesar estimated a large vehicle, at least one that carried a heavy load.

Sounds of grinding wheels faded away. Cesar listened for the vehicle's return trip from the turnaround. After a few minutes, the boy sat up and swung his leg off the bed. He picked up the flip phone at his bedside and opened it. The blank display cast a faint light and his foot found his sandal. He tugged on a T-shirt and grabbed his crutch, and stuffed the flip phone in the front pocket of his jeans.

Cesar moved quietly through the house and slipped out the front door. The light outside was better. The moon was a waning silver crescent, but the sky was clear and the road shone like a white river under a lacework of stars.

Cesar crutch-walked toward the cove. He peered into the darkness and discerned the linear contours of a box truck parked at the turnaround. Cesar drew closer and saw several shadowy figures moving behind the truck. He left the road and crept toward the bluff to gain a better angle, and saw the glow of lights in the cove. He crawled to the edge of the cliff, dragging his crutch.

In the middle of the cove, a 40-foot white boat idled. Its rear deck was well lit and a tight spotlight was trained on the beach. Off to Cesar's left, several men in dark clothing unloaded plastic-wrapped bundles the size of sofa pillows from the box truck and toted them down the narrow path to the beach, finding their way with tiny flashlights. The men set the bundles on the shore and climbed back up the path.

An inflatable dinghy containing two more men motored from the white boat to the beach. The men loaded the bundles and ferried them back. Two more men on the white boat received the bundles and carried them into the cabin. Their movements were purposeful and efficient; no time or motion was wasted.

A husky man stood in the surf with two bundles under his arms. An incoming surge lifted and dipped the white boat and the spotlight danced over the man's face. Cesar ducked down. The man standing in the surf was Ramiro Ramos.

When Cesar looked up again the spotlight had steadied and Ramos was handing bundles off to the men in the inflatable. He relayed two more bundles from the beach to the dinghy and climbed back up the path.

Ramos and the two men from the truck carried the last bundles to the shore. Ramos stepped into the dinghy and motored to the white boat. After the bundles were transferred Ramos and the men boarded. They attached the dinghy to a hoist and raised it out of the water, and the spotlight went dark. The two men entered the cabin and Ramos remained on the deck. Cesar turned and watched the box truck drive up the road and go over the rise.

The white boat's inboard motor gunned and water boiled behind the stern. A man wearing a natty suit, white fedora and aviator sunglasses emerged from the cabin.

Detective Barojas spoke to Ramos, but Cesar could not hear his words. Two men burst out of the cabin carrying machine guns and stood behind Barojas. Ramos stepped back, waving his hands and shaking his head.

Barojas raised a handgun from his side. A silencer extended from the barrel. Ramos backed to the rail and Barojas' muzzle flashed. Ramos doubled over and clutched his gut, then rolled over the side of the boat. Barojas stepped to the rail and the muzzle flashed twice more, and Ramos lay still in the foaming wake, face down.

Barojas gazed at Ramos' inert form as he unscrewed his silencer. He opened his jacket and holstered his gun. The men with machine guns returned to the cabin and the white boat pulled away.

Barojas remained on the rear deck and held onto the canopy's aluminum frame. He turned toward the bluff and fixed his gaze on the cliff where Cesar lay. The boy felt exposed, even in the darkness, and he backed away from the edge. Barojas was still staring toward Cesar when the white boat left the cove and turned north.

Cesar crept to the cliff's edge and saw the shadowy form of Ramos floating on the still surface of the cove. Ramos' body spasmed and ripples glimmered, and Cesar heard him gasp for air. The boy pulled himself up on his crutch and started home. Torn by competing impulses of vengeance and duty, he paused. He listened for Abuelito's wise counsel but none came. I need you, Abuelito, he thought. Where are you?

Cesar returned to the cliff and saw Ramos thrash in the water. He hurried to the turnaround and abandoned his crutch, and scooted down the path to the cove, his hands and foot finding familiar holds as he made his way.

On the sand, Cesar hopped to the cleft in the bluff. He reached in and found the smooth edge of the longboard. He tugged the longboard out of the cleft and tucked the front end under his arm, and hopped to the water's edge, dragging the longboard behind him. The boy flung it on the water and lay on top, and paddled into the cove, still hoping Abuelito would advise him to turn back.

Cesar heard Ramos cough and he paddled toward the sound. He came upon Ramos just as he slipped below the surface. Cesar rotated the longboard and scanned the water. A massive hand pierced the surface. Ramos clutched the tip of the longboard and pulled himself up, almost launching the boy into the water. When he saw Cesar, Ramos said, "You stupid kid."

Ramos pulled his way along the edge of the longboard toward Cesar and the boy retreated to the end of the board. "Wait—I can help you," Cesar said.

Ramos lunged for the boy. Cesar splashed into the water and clung to the back of the longboard. Ramos lunged again and caught Cesar's T-shirt. The boy flailed his arms, but Ramos' grip was strong.

Ramos pulled Cesar close and said, "You can't help me, kid. I've been dead for a long time." He flung the boy on top of the longboard. "But you aren't."

Ramos pointed the longboard toward the shore. "Go save the world, kid," he said, and shoved the board hard.

Cesar paddled with all his strength and paused only when he was within reach of the beach. He swung his left leg into the surf and planted his foot in the sand, and leaned over the longboard, panting.

He looked back at the placid surface of the cove and saw no movement. The boy stilled his breathing and listened, but only the mellow rhythm of small, breaking waves creased the silence of the night.

28

The next morning Ramos' body was discovered floating outside the cove by a catamaran charter. By noon, official vehicles lined both sides of the village's single-lane road, from crest to turnaround. A parade of federal police, investigators in suits, and men wearing black ski masks tromped up and down the road. Several TV news vehicles vied for what little parking space remained.

Rosa watched the official activity from her doorway and asked a passing officer what the commotion was about. The officer said someone had been murdered. "You should stay inside, señora. The killer may still be in the area."

During his recovery Cesar had taken to sleeping well past sunrise and Rosa accepted his new sleeping habits as a byproduct of his leg injury. When he didn't rise by noon she looked in his room and saw her son lying on his bed in his green T-shirt and board shorts, staring at the ceiling. His jeans lay on the floor. Rosa picked them up and hung them on a hook behind the door, and sat on his bed.

"How long have you been awake?" she asked.

"A long time."

"Don't you hear all the cars? There must be at least twenty."

"I hear them."

"Somebody was killed. Federal police are everywhere. Some are wearing scary masks. I think they're looking for clues."

"Did they find any?"

"I don't know."

A knock sounded at the front door. Cesar flinched and his eyes widened.

Rosa left the room and opened the door. She was greeted by officers Ruiz and Diaz.

"Do you and the boy have a couple minutes, señora?" Ruiz asked.

"Can you tell me what's going on?"

"A man was murdered somewhere around here last night," Diaz said. "Shot at close range. Know anything about it?"

"Me? No. I mean, why would I?"

"We believe it was the same man who murdered your father," Ruiz said.

Rosa caught her breath and her hand went to her mouth.

Diaz said, "Small world that he should be gunned down so close to your home."

"I'm shocked. I know nothing about it."

"Is your son home?"

"Cesar, can you come out here?"

Cesar emerged from his room and stood next to Rosa, leaning on his crutch.

"A man was killed near here last night," Diaz said. "Probably the same man who killed your grandfather."

Diaz studied Cesar's face but observed no reaction.

"Do either of you have a gun?"

"Cesar has never touched a gun," Rosa said. "How dare you suggest that my son was anywhere near one."

"Please come with us."

Cesar and Rosa followed the officers to a police car. Diaz opened the back door and said to Cesar, "Have a seat."

"Are you arresting my son?"

"Why? Should I?"

Rosa took Cesar's crutch and the boy flopped into the back seat. A dozen officers gathered around the car.

Diaz crouched in front of Cesar. "I saw you on TV, Cesar. You are one brave boy. Can you be brave for me one more time?" Cesar eyed the officer warily.

"The man who killed your grandpa was executed somewhere around here last night, maybe early this morning. Know anything about that? Anything that could help us solve the case so everyone can go home?"

Rosa tilted her head back defiantly. "He was home all night. I would know if he went out."

"Señora, I'm not suggesting that your son had anything to do with it. I just need to ask a few questions. Strictly routine."

Rosa crossed her arms. "Ask your questions."

"Do you own a surfboard, Cesar? A blue surfboard?"

"He owns a blue surfboard," Rosa said. "So what? Many people own blue surfboards."

"Is that true, Cesar?"

"Yes."

"Did you use it recently?"

"No." Cesar looked away and felt Diaz' dubious gaze.

"Did you use it yesterday? Or maybe last night?"

Rosa cocked her hand on her hip. "My son does not lie. I raised him right."

"I need to inspect you for cuts. Please hold out your hands and arms."

Diaz examined the boy.

"Please take off your shirt."

Cesar pulled up the bottom of his T-shirt. Officer Diaz's eyes narrowed at the sight of the scars on the boy's chest.

Rosa tugged Cesar's T-shirt back down. "Who do you think you are, putting my son through this nonsense? I want to speak to your boss."

Officers standing behind Diaz moved aside. A tall, gaunt man wearing a white fedora stepped behind Diaz. Cesar looked up and saw his amber reflection in Detective Barojas' aviator sunglasses.

"Step away señora or I'll have you arrested for interfering," Diaz said. Her eyes burned and she bit her lip. Diaz glared at Cesar. "Now answer me. You used your surfboard last night, didn't you?"

"I was home all night."

"Suppose you tell me how blood got on your surfboard. Last time I checked, surfboards don't bleed."

Cesar and Barojas locked eyes.

"Simple question," Diaz said. "We'll discuss it at the

police station, if that's what you want to do."

"That will be enough," Barojas said. "There is no connection between the boy and the events of last night."

Diaz stood and faced Barojas. "With respect, sir, the boy isn't being entirely—"

Barojas leaned close to the officer and growled through clenched teeth. "Are you challenging my judgment?"

"No, sir."

"We'll discuss it at the police station, if that's what you want to do."

"No, sir." Diaz turned and marched away. Ruiz puffed his cheeks and blew, and followed the younger officer at a distance.

Barojas turned to Cesar. "You and your mama go home. No one will bother you again."

"Thank you, detective," Rosa said. "They are like animals."

"Yes, and some of them bite."

"Will they catch the killer?"

"That is doubtful, señora. The cartels—and I'm not saying they had a hand in this—the cartels are smart. They cover their tracks."

"Such a frightening thought."

"You should take your son away from this place. They may come back."

"The cartel?"

"The police."

"Thank you, detective."

"Be safe." Barojas turned and walked away.

By evening Rosa and Cesar had packed the Chrysler with everything they could fit. Cesar looked around his little house and Abuelito's annex one last time and joined his mother in front of the house.

The sun was low and only a few vehicles remained. Barojas stood in front of his sedan near the bluff and spoke with several officers. Rosa sat in the front seat of the Chrysler and started the car.

Cesar walked toward Barojas.

Rosa rolled down her window. "Cesar, it's time to go."

"One minute."

Detective Barojas and the officers saw Cesar approach and stopped talking.

"I see that you and your mama are leaving," Barojas said. "That is a wise decision."

Cesar handed a folded paper to Barojas as Rosa drove up in the Chrysler. Cesar joined his mother in the front seat and the car pulled away.

Barojas unfolded the paper, a flyer given by the students to Cesar and Abuelito at the harbor. The headline read, "Stopping Ocean Pollution Starts with You."

Rosa turned on her headlights as she cruised south on the coast road. Cesar stared out the window, lost in thought. His crutch rested between his legs.

Rosa pulled the Chrysler onto the shoulder of the road in front of a school bus stop. She opened the trunk and pulled out boxes of sporting goods from Cesar's bedroom, and set them on the bench. She laid the hockey stick on top of the boxes.

Rosa returned to the car and proceeded south. "Thanks," Cesar said. He reached into a pocket and withdrew Abuelito's savings, and handed the roll of bills to his mother.

"Where did you get this?" Rosa asked, her wide eyes swinging between her son and the thick wad of bills. "It's a lot of money."

"Abuelito saved it so we could catch a blue marlin on a white boat. We caught one so I don't need the money."

Rosa tucked the cash in her purse, which lay by her side.

"I have something for you." Rosa fished Cesar's flip phone out of her purse and handed it to the boy. He opened the phone. Wet sand sprinkled on his lap and water spread under the black display. He pressed the power button but the display remained dark.

"It was in your pants pocket. Maybe it went for a swim while you were sleeping last night."

Cesar closed his eyes and leaned his head back, and smiled.

The hills above Cesar's village emitted a golden glow as the sun dipped behind the ocean horizon. The old man smiled and gave the pull cord a yank. The Evinrude hummed.

Abuelito grasped the tiller and turned the skiff west, and motored toward the setting sun.

The End